mmw

CONTENTS

New Millennium Writings, Issue 28, 2019

WRITING AWARDS + NEWS

NEW MILLENNIUM WRITINGS

POETRY SUITE 2019

CONTRIBUTORS

THE BACK MATTERS

The editors and judges at

NEW MILLENNIUM WRITINGS

are pleased to announce the

45TH NEW MILLENNIUM POETRY AWARD

XIAO YUE (SHELLY) SHAN

of Tokyo, Japan

"THE NATION OF APHASIA"

POETRY FINALISTS | AWARDS XLV

Kemmer Anderson, Chattanooga, Tennessee... "Ancient Addictions"

Constance Campana, Attleboro, Massachusetts..."Incident, 2015"

Jack Cooper, Eugene, Oregon..."By Way of Crying"

James Cooper, Carmichael, California..."Clinical Note Template for Men in Therapy"

Lisa Dordal, Nashville, Tennessee..."Welcome"

C.W. Emerson, Los Angeles, California..."Stopover on a Road Trip to L.A., 1981"

Ed Frankel, Forestville, California..."Gueluegetza"

Sam Griswold, Ossining, New York..."The House I Wish I Grew Up In"

Michele Harris, Cambridge, Massachusetts..."Instinct"

Sandy Longley, Delmar, New York..."Solace at the P.O."

Damen O'Brien, Wynnum, Queensland, Australia..."The Darkness"

Yvonne Reddick, Manchester, United Kingdom..."Muirburn"

Victoria Richards, London, United Kingdom..."Weaning"

Lois Roma-Deeley, Scottsdale, Arizona..."Why Moon Jellyfish Won't Speak of Cancer"

Anne Sandor, Monroe, New York..."Ossuaries"

Heidi Seaborn, Seattle, Washington..."Dress Up"

Sophia Stid, Nashville, Tennessee..."The Marriage Bed"

Allen Sweat, West Palm Beach, Florida..."Riding the Dream"

John Sibley Williams, Milwaukie, Oregon..."It's only an island if you look at it from the water"

Keith Woodruff, Akron, Ohio..."Hot Mess"

The editors and judges at

NEW MILLENNIUM WRITINGS

are pleased to announce the

46TH NEW MILLENNIUM POETRY AWARD

SETH SIMONS

of the Bay Area, California

"LIKE MY FATHER"

POETRY FINALISTS | AWARDS XLVI

Alice Ashe, Decatur , GA..."some things that come in twos"

Jacqueline Berger, San Francisco , CA..."Moral Injury"

FJ Bergmann, Madison , WI..."This Time"

Sarah Blanchard, Raleigh , NC..."Optative Dreaming"

Shuyu Cao, North Hollywood , CA..."Slave"

C.W. Emerson, Los Angeles , CA..."After Visiting the Lourdes of Lebanon"

Robert Evory, Portage , MI..."Sympathy Vibration"

Elizabeth Jackson, Raleigh , NC..."Constellations"

Trish Lindsey Jaggers, Smiths Grove , KY..." Migrant "

A. Kaiser, Brooklyn , NY..."At the speed of light, squared"

Barbara Mossberg, Eugene , OR..."When I Die You Don't Have to Divert the River for Me"

Terri Niccum, Buena Park , CA..."Creosote Bush"

Laura Polley, French Lick , IN..."Symbiotic"

Marjorie Saiser, Green Valley , AZ..."In the Time of the Great Forgetters"

Joyce Schmid, Palo Alto , CA..."Phone Calls"

Mark Scott, Allen , TX..."Love Poem"

Bracha Sharp, Bronx , NY..."Words"

Kurt Steinwand, Brandon , FL..."Occupation"

Jim Glenn Thatcher, Yarmouth , ME..."The Drunken Novel"

Barbara Ungar, Saratoga Springs , NY..."The Last Jaguar"

The editors and judges at

NEW MILLENNIUM WRITINGS

are pleased to announce the

45TH NEW MILLENNIUM FLASH FICTION AWARD

ALYSON HAGY

of Laramie, Wyoming

"EMBER"

FLASH FICTION FINALISTS | AWARDS XLV

Julia Barclay, New York, New York..."1965"

Kelly Bedbrook, Waterloo, Ontario..."Thirty-six"

Charles Booth, Oak Harbor, Washington..."On the Occasion of Burying My Neighbor's Dog"

Maloy Das, London, United Kingdom..."The Part about the Plankton"

Jean Ende, Brooklyn, New York..."The Best Is Yet To Be"

Roberta Gates, Riverside, Illinois..."Fraternity Row"

Sheryl Goodspeed, Torrance, California..."He Looks at the Earth, and It Trembles"

Kate Hanson, Nashville, Tennessee..."The Lost and Found"

Timothy Hillmer, Louisville, Colorado..."Stones and Soap"

Michelle Hsu, Studio City, California..."Bus Depot"

Ella Jacobson, Brooklyn, New York..."The Things They Loved"

Rose Kinney, Hattiesburg, Mississippi..."John Waters Is Following Me"

John Lankford, Ranchos De Taos, New Mexico..."Forgotten Words"

Andrea Martin, Chicago, Illinois..."The Peace Plan"

Suzanne Mattaboni, Northampton, Pennsylvania..."The Hood of the Camry"

Becky Ruff, Prairie du Chien, Wisconsin..."These Three Remain"

Jonathan Segol, Saratoga Springs, New York..."Livewire"

Judith Shaw, Bolinas, California..."Her"

Kate Simonian, Lubbock, Texas..."Mothlight"

Bonnie West, Saint Paul, Minnesota..."Book by Book"

The editors and judges at

NEW MILLENNIUM WRITINGS

are pleased to announce the

46TH NEW MILLENNIUM FLASH FICTION AWARD

ELEANOR BLUESTEIN

of La Jolla, California

"HOW TO WRITE A LOVE LETTER"

FLASH FICTION FINALISTS | AWARDS XLVI

Beth Balousek, Monroe, New York..."Fission"

David Carren, Edinburg, Texas..."A Can and a Pint"

Clare Gardner, Abu Dhabi, U.A.E...."Exigua"

Judy Geraci, San Diego, California..."Messy Things"

Carlos Gomez, Forest Hills, New York..."Intersection"

Ruth Joffre, Seattle, Washington..."A Girl Climbs a Tree"

Thea Kinyon Boodhoo, San Francisco, California..."Incredible"

Kathleen McNamara, Rimrock, Arizona..."Benediction for Cheryl"

Frazer Merritt, Cambridge, United Kingdon..."Dark Epiphany"

Courtney Morris, Black River, Jamaica..."10:53 PM"

Carolyn Ogburn, Marshall, North Carolina..."Before You Were Born"

Ellen Perry, Weaverville, North Carolina..."Medusa"

Tracy Robert, Newport Beach, California..."Pedagogy"

Collin Segura, Aiken, South Carolina..."A Woman's Best Friend"

Reena Shah, Brooklyn, New York..."Hari Om Senior Center"

Kate Simonian, Lubbock, Texas..."Moving Out"

Morgan Smith, Santa Fe, New Mexico..."Where's Jason?"

Carl Thompson Jr., Gainesville, Virginia..."In an Outdoor Market"

Kate Whitehead, Toronto, Canada..."Stuart's Mine"

A. E. Wynter, Mankato, Minnesota..."The Things My Afro Knows"

The editors and judges at

NEW MILLENNIUM WRITINGS

are pleased to announce the

45TH NEW MILLENNIUM FICTION AWARD

PATRICK DAWSON

of London, England

"THE LANGUAGE OF RIVERS"

FICTION FINALISTS | AWARDS XLV

Colin Brezicki, Niagara-on-the-Lake, Ontario, Canada..."An Original Sin"

Jackie Davis Martin, San Francisco, California..."Workout"

Sally Lipton Derringer, Nanuet, New York..."Medals"

Brian Feehan, Wilton, Connecticut..."For Him"

Barbara Ganley, Weybridge, Vermont..."When Hippies Move In"

Amina Gautier, Chicago, Illinois..."Hungry, Like the Wolf"

Amalia Gladhart, Eugene, Oregon..."Misdirection"

Adam Golub, Fullerton, California..."The Silver Lake Bandit"

Scott Lambridis, Placerville, California..."A Problem of Lighting"

Alfred Marks, Sydney, New South Wales, Australia..."Flights"

Suzanne Mattaboni, Northampton, Pennsylvania..."Cartoons"

Liza Mattison, Stow, Massachusetts..."The Codes of Moral Conduct"

Rashaan Meneses, Berkeley, California..."Ghosts for Water"

Peter Newall, Armidale, New South Wales, Australia..."A Box of Photographs"

Laura Rocha, Bellaire, Texas..."Safe Travel in Bear Country"

Connie Corzilius Spasser, Augusta, Georgia..."Mary Beth"

Maureen Tobin-Stanley, Duluth, Minnesota..."Igor Eye"

J.L. Torres, Plattsburgh, New York..."Rip and Reck Into That Good Light"

Cynthia Walker, Santa Barbara, California..."An Interested Party"

R. S. Wynn, Dresden, Maine..."Basement Miracles"

The editors and judges at

New Millennium Writings

are pleased to announce the

46TH NEW MILLENNIUM FICTION AWARD

Patricia Sammon

of Huntsville, Alabama

"SINCE"

Fiction finalists | Awards XLVI

Teresa Burns Gunther, Oakland, California..."Lilies"

Margaret Collier, Espoo, Finland..."Emergency Contact of Santa Claus"

David Connor, Los Angeles, California..."Around the Parking Lot"

Corinne Dwyer, Clearwater, Minnesota..."The Last Migration"

Shanteé Felix, Baltimore, Maryland..."A Woman of a Certain Hue"

H.E. Francis, Huntsville, Alabama..."Put Yourself in My Hands"

Roberta Gates, Riverside, Illinois..."Goodbye, Savannah"

Doris Iarovici, Boston, Massachusetts..."One Way It Could Happen"

Mel Konner, Avondale Estates, Georgia..."Blessings"

Frank Meola, Brooklyn, New York..."Home as Found"

Mil Norman-Risch, Richmond, Virginia..."Predator"

Terri Scullen, Alexandria, Virginia..."Wetlands"

Marylou Streznewski, Furlong, Pennsylvania..."In the Eye of the Great Staring Moon"

Santiago Vaquera-Vásquez, Albuquerque, New Mexico..."Sometimes A Steady Light"

Cady Vishniac, Ann Arbor, Michigan..."Justice Is a Myth"

John E. White, Altadena, California..."Castle Green Parakeet"

Paul Wilborn, Saint Petersburg, Florida..."Smoke"

Juliet Wittman, Boulder, Colorado..."Elisa"

Aaron Wood, Charleston, South Carolina..."When They Came"

Sandra Worsham, Milledgeville, Georgia..."The Washer's Husband"

The editors and judges at

NEW MILLENNIUM WRITINGS

are pleased to announce the

45TH NEW MILLENNIUM NONFICTION AWARD

MARSH ROSE

of Cloverdale, California

"FALSE MEMORY"

NONFICTION FINALISTS | AWARDS XLV

Katie Barnes, Nashville, Tennessee..."The Domino Effect"

Dawn-Michelle Baude, Las Vegas, Nevada..."Cleaver Residence, 105 Lamoine Lane"

Cherline Bazile, Cambridge, Massachusetts..."Walking Text"

Rosie Cohan, Berkeley, California..."Hassan's Wedding Celebration"

Sage Cohen, Portland, Oregon..."Cloud Bed"

Raphael Dagold, Baltimore, Maryland..."Injury"

David Gehring, Seattle, Washington..."Verona"

Robert Kirvel, Clayton, California..."Four Scenes and the Problem of Intermediate Gray"

Marissa Korbel, Portland, Oregon..."Ways of Being Seen"

Amy Long, Miramar Beach, Florida..."Product Warning"

Saffron Marchant, Pokfulam, Hong Kong..."Midwife's Daughter"

J. Jacqueline McLean, Minneapolis, Minnesota..."The Project Lie"

Natalie Mucker, Highland Heights, Kentucky..."A Week of Unwell"

Mary Pfeiffer, Plano, Texas..."Searching for Aunt Sarah"

Mickey Revenaugh, Brooklyn, New York..."Choppers"

Johanna Rossi, Newburyport, Massachusetts..."Something Came Looking for Me"

Katie Simon, Somerville, Massachusetts..."Paint"

Judith Hannah Weiss, Scottsville, Virginia..."Brain Drain"

Bradley Wester, Bristol, Rhode Island..."Brothers Katrina"

The editors and judges at

NEW MILLENNIUM WRITINGS

are pleased to announce the

46TH NEW MILLENNIUM NONFICTION AWARD

KRISTIN KOSTICK

of Houston, Texas

"BLANKING"

NONFICTION FINALISTS | AWARDS XLVI

Susanna Barlow, Bluffdale, Utah..."House of Storm"

Joanna Brichetto, Nashville, Tennessee..."A Dandelion Is to Blow"

Jenifer Campo, El Dorado Hills, California..."Blind Faith"

Britt Cannon, Brooklyn, New York..."Trippin' Through The Trees"

Christina Cha, San Francisco, California..."Where You Were Raped and Murdered"

Judith Dancoff, Los Angeles, California..."My Father, the Atomic Bomb"

Alicia Ezekiel-Pipkin, Orlando, Florida..."The Silver Warden and Its Martyrs"

Jeri Griffith, Brattleboro, Vermont..."Logos"

Kacie Main, Jacksonville Beach, Florida..."The Battle"

Sybil McLain-Topel, Chattanooga, Tennessee..."A Bike Ride from Grayton Beach"

J. Jacqueline McLean, Minneapolis, Minnesota..."Can't Cha, don't Cha"

Rosemary Needham-Curtis, Camden, Maine..."Wild Ocean"

Sharon Osborn, Haven, New Jersey..."Saving Grace"

Jean Ann Pollard, Winslow, Maine..."Seminar"

Morgan Smith, Santa Fe, New Mexico..."One Eyed in Juárez"

A. Louise Staman, Savannah, Georgia..."Glenn Frank: An Unexpected Hero"

Sharon Swanson, Chapel Hill, North Carolina..."Free Fall All Over Again"

Andrew Weinstein, Brooklyn, New York..."The Bridge"

Howard Williams, San Francisco, California..."Wag the Dog at 20: Sex, Lies and Video Wars"

Judith Yarrow, Seattle, Washington..."I Met an Octopus on My Way to Alpha Centauri"

The editors and judges at

NEW MILLENNIUM WRITINGS

are excited to announce the new

Litteratura Influentia Award

KRISTIN KOSTICK

of Houston, Texas

"DISAPPEARED"

THE **LITTERATURA INFLUENTIA AWARD** IS RESERVED FOR REMARKABLE DISPLAYS OF LITERARY COURAGE AND ARTISTRY WHICH TRAIL-BLAZE IN DARKNESS AND SHINE LIGHT UPON PREVIOUSLY UNSEEN, UNKNOWN, AND UNEXPECTED PIECES OF OUR HUMAN CONDITION

This important award will be bestowed no more than twice per year. Everyone who submits to *NMW* is eligible. Stories, essays, and poems are eligible. The decision process does not begin until all first place awards have been chosen and confirmed.

English Translation

The Influence of Literature

The editors and judges at

NEW MILLENNIUM WRITINGS

are excited to announce the new

NEW MILLENNIUM NEW WRITER AWARD

COMING SOON

Beginning in 2020, all submissions from new and emerging writers — who have never won a First Place writing award and have never published a full-length book — will be eligible for the NEW MILLENNIUM NEW WRITER AWARD.

DEDICATION

The Kings Bay Plowshares 7 face decades in prison for exposing illegal and immoral nuclear weapons that threaten all life on Earth. These seven people nonviolently and symbolically disarmed the Trident nuclear submarine base at Kings Bay, GA on April 4, 2018, the 50th anniversary of the assassination of Martin Luther King, Jr.

At the trial, defendants were prohibited from using key evidence and from sharing their motivations. Four expert witnesses, including former National Security Council member, Daniel Ellsberg, were not allowed to testify. In his most recent book, *The Doomsday Machine: Confessions of a Nuclear War Planner*, Ellsberg points out that as few as 10 nuclear missiles, out of a US arsenal of 2000 warheads, could destroy all human life on earth.

One Trident submarine is nearly two football fields long, can carry 24 submarine-launched ballistic missiles, with each missile capable of carrying eight W88 nuclear warheads.

14: Kilotons dropped on Hiroshima

150,000: People killed by the atomic bombing of Hiroshima

455: Kilotons on ONE W88 warhead

3,640: Maximum kilotons on ONE missile

87,360: Maximum kilotons on ONE Trident submarine

345,600: Total kilotons deployed on Trident fleet

The United States currently has 14 Trident ballistic-missile submarines.

Read their indictment on page 199, along with ways to help.

New Millennium
WRITINGS

mmw

DISAPPEARED

Kristin Kostick

That summer in Vegas, kids were disappearing left and right. Stories came out every week in the news about kidnappings, flash floods sweeping kids from drainage ditches, kids last seen at gas stations or truck stops and never heard from again. Their missing faces were plastered in the usual places: milk cartons, backs of trucks, telephone poles, bulletin boards at the grocery store. *Have you seen me?* You got the sense that you, too, could just slip away at any moment, the whole of you reduced to a fog or a breeze. It was 1989, the days before TV and video games were go-to forms of play, when parents told their kids to "go play outside." My parents didn't much care what my brother and I did, as long as we stayed out of trouble. Lee and I banded together with the other neighborhood kids—Tim and his sister Teresa, and Lindsay, the socially awkward only child who lived at the far end of the cul-de-sac—to wander through the dusty undeveloped lots in a clearing behind our houses, kicking over scraps of metal or cardboard to scavenge for a makeshift clubhouse. Every so

New Millennium Writings, Issue 28, 2019

often, we came across grubby copies of *Hustler* or *Penthouse* or *Club* left in the dirt, and in the heat of the morning we'd huddle around, flipping and staring into the stiff, grimy pages. None of us dared take them home. Our unspoken agreement was that whatever we did out there in the frontier of that construction site—ghosted-out with the foreign and terrifying relics of adulthood abandoned in the dirt—remained separate from what we did in the streets of our own neighborhood: roller-skating, riding bikes, swimming in each other's pools. Our cul-de-sac was our playground, safely quarantined from the bad stories we heard on the nightly news, from the abductions, from the stabbings and shootings down on the Strip near Fremont Street. The edge of our neighborhood marked an implicit boundary.

But just beyond it lay our construction zone, that dry expanse of desert where our imaginations were free to run wild, detached from parents and homework, those casual reinforcements of reality. The construction itself seemed to have ceased temporarily, as if the city had mysteriously called off any progress. It seemed to exist all the more, then, just for us, our miniature version of the Western frontier. The enormous lot was far enough away to constitute a kind of unleashing, where we sensed the rules were different, though we didn't yet know how. Even the dirt looked different, loosened and upturned instead of orderly and compact as in our neighborhood garden landscapes with their choreographed cacti. But the lot was also close enough, we thought, to come back home whenever we wanted, which made it our sacred in-between place, a testing ground.

For the better part of one morning, Lee and Tim tried to start the engine of a tractor sitting in the middle of the clearing. No one else was around. They scrambled up the side and into the tractor's cockpit, staring in bewilderment at the overwhelming array of levers and unlabeled knobs and switches, controls that looked like appendages of some unfamiliar beast, with the capacity to unlock the huge mechanical arm, the monstrous forward-moving treads. The boys were freaked out, curious; they started flipping levers, seeing what might happen. Either with a left-behind key or enigmatic knob, they got the motor started and the whole atrocious machine rumbled to life under their skinny legs, the claw-like arm traveling up and down, the tractor treads shifting forward in the dirt.

Terrified, they leapt from the tractor, abandoning it mid-life. In an attempt to shut off the engine, Tim shoved a paper towel in the tractor's air intake. *Cut off the beast's breath. Kill it before it kills you*! He must have heard that somewhere—in a movie or a comic book. Whether on account of the towel or some other mystery of the engine, the tractor sputtered to a stop and the claw arm thudded into the dirt with defeat. Shaken up, the boys ran from the construction site, weaving through the roads back to our cul-de-sac, already reformulating in their minds how to exaggerate the story for the rest of us. *It was like a monster! It was after us, trying to eat us alive!*

After the tractor incident, Lee and Tim stayed away from the big machines, stuck to the certain inertness of the scraps. But then something else began to unfold, something better than the tractor, better than anything that had come before, the boys told us. One afternoon, back at the construction site, after an hour or two of kicking around in the dirt, they found a clearing they decided would be the perfect spot to tunnel out a fort. They had gotten their hands on a shovel, probably stolen from my dad's garage. Trading it back and forth, they dug hard into the dirt, more like dried clay, heaving small clumps of desert on to the ground behind them. Before long, they had dug over a foot down. Then a foot and a half. At this rate, the fort would take forever. But the boys knew it was possible. My dad had said one night over dinner that there were immense cave systems out in the desert and no one knew where they led. Maybe the miners had made them in the days of the Old West. Maybe outlaws used them to store stolen riches and hooch, to hide their helpless captives. *Maybe that's where all the kids are going*, I had suggested, flattening my peas into a perfect green savannah.

The shovel suddenly hit something not-dirt. Something was *down there*, something the boys hadn't been looking for. But what could be buried in the middle of an empty construction lot? The fact that they had come across something buried in the exact spot where they had been digging out their fort made it seem plausible to the boys that they were destined to find whatever it was.

After digging out around it and leaning into the hole to grab ahold, they hauled the object out with their four hands and plopped it on the ground. They stared down at it. Square. Fake leather. A handle. A briefcase? They squatted down to fumble with the rolling combination, but it was locked. They hovered over it, as if waiting for it to auto-resuscitate. To them, this was not just a briefcase. It was a vision, a vessel containing the utterly unknown, the kind of treasure we had all what-iffed about after watching movies like *The Goonies* and *The Neverending Story*. Sure, it was dingy and caked in dry desert earth, but as they exchanged glances the boys knew it was certain to contain riches, gold bullion, straight from some heist, maybe a cache of neatly stacked hundred-dollar bills. Or jewels! Stolen diamonds, precious sapphire. The mafiosos might be coming up from their downtown casinos any minute to reclaim it. "We have to break it open," my brother said.

Lee and Tim never budged from the original way they told it, that the briefcase really had been buried exactly where they had started digging. When the boys later told us, all of us sitting cross-legged on the sidewalk at the half-way point of our cul-de-sac, we said there was no way that could be true. Too much of a coincidence. The boys were either making it up, or something else was going on. But what? We started thinking up possible explanations, thinking anything might be possible there. That place was out of our jurisdiction, could operate under rules of nature we had never fathomed. Teresa said maybe the quality of dirt in that spot, having been dug up once before, looked subconsciously more diggable, softer somehow. I suggested that maybe there was something magnetic about the spot that attracted our brains through ESP. Lindsay's contribution was to try to stifle her giggles long enough to say something, but she couldn't.

What was in it?! I imagine that as we leaned forward, our circle looked from above like a flower closing its bloom.

With a rock or a wrench from the construction lot, Lee and Tim had hacked away at the cheap, faux-gold lock until it smithereened. This was it, the defining moment. Opening with painstaking caution, they anticipated the amber light of gold reflected upon their cheeks, or the sparkle of diamonds against the background of dirt. But what if it was a severed arm, or a dead animal? They were both prepared and not prepared for anything.

The lid made a dry cracking sound when they leaned it back to peer inside. Here was their treasure trove, what they had toiled so long to excavate. Their shaky hands reached towards the contents, unsure whether to make physical contact. There they sat, stacks and stacks of crusty, ripped, mangled porn magazines from the 1970s and '80s, pushed against the case's lining, unkempt, as if someone had stashed them away quickly, getting rid of the evidence in a hurry. The boys looked down it in disbelief. It couldn't be just this, there must be something more. The pages were brittle, curled up at the edges. With pinched fingers, they picked up the magazines one by one, hoping something might be underneath them all, deep at the remote bottom of the suitcase, a payoff for their scrupulous toils. They pawed their way to the briefcase's lining, casting the magazines out one by one. Once they all lay in a heap of sullied paper on the dirt, the boys peered down into the briefcase's empty shell, the inside fabric a little frayed, smelling of mildew.

The milk-carton kids were different every week, sometimes multiple kids on different cartons within a few days. Why not put their faces on cigarette packs or boxes of donuts, objects of consumption for people who might actually be capable of finding them? Merely kids ourselves, we felt helpless to do anything but memorize the others' faces, look around at other girls and boys in the grocery stores and movie theatres wondering: *Could she be the one from this week? Will I see his face in a month or two?* Teresa and Lindsay and I considered saving all the cut-out heads and making a collage, or a game where we could somehow match them by distinctive features into some revelatory pattern. The whole enterprise of trying to find the kids seemed futile, an elaborate farce to make the parents of the missing ones believe they might one day be found.

In a way, we all participated in the lie. In the mornings, I slurped spoonful after spoonful of cereal and scrutinized the smiling face on the carton. I tried to picture the child wearing a different expression, maybe wide-eyed with shock and fear in the midst of capture, or weeping alone in the darkness of some van or improvised dungeon. But in my imagination, I could only picture again and again the same disturbing image. It was of the kid-of-the-week stumbling around in the desert with the milk-carton cut-out of its smiling paper head balanced on its shoulders, like a stick-figure or a Potato-Head doll. I could not picture them all as real. That was too scary. With the rest of the city, I pretended they were really out there somewhere, with their real heads, their real mouths shaping the repetitive *o* in *home, bring me home.*

Maybe it was the backdrop of these stories, or the sheer eeriness of that vast, deserted construction zone that imbued the whole summer with a feeling that, just beyond the edges of what we could see, something perilous lurked, lying dormant. Even something about the sunlight, gleaming off the abandoned tractors and metal scraps, seemed decidedly spooky, like light from another distant world invading our own. Over the rooftops we could make out the jagged mountains framing our valley, containing our city. Beyond that, more and more desert, a world of spiky, armored plants and animals we knew better from imagination than observation.

One day Lee and Tim led us girls out to the construction zone. The boys had finally built the fort. We looked out over the clearing, nothing visible but dirt and more dirt, the tractor, and some discarded scraps of wood and cardboard.

"You can't see it from the surface," Lee said. We followed them, our grubby sneakers padding over the ground, to a dusty wooden pallet lying in the dirt. Lee bent down to lift it with two scrawny arms, revealing a small, black hole mined into the ground. Lindsay erupted with giddy laughter, and Teresa and I stepped back, amazed. The boys, not hiding their pride, watched our surprise with delight. "You guys built… a *cave*?" I asked.

The four of us scooted down the hole along a makeshift ladder and came to sit shoulder-to-shoulder on the dirt floor of a three-by-three-foot crawlspace. It was pitch black, save for the stream of light cutting through from above. Particles of dust whirled about our heads. The ceiling was held up by cardboard boxes and wooden armatures to keep the space from falling in on itself. We craned our necks toward the dim walls and ceiling to see that every inch of the fort's interior was covered with the brittle magazine clippings of naked women sprawled with their high-heeled feet angled upwards or outwards, their '70s-era hairstyles framing erotic expressions, lips parted to voice a barely audible *Ohhh*, eyes half-mast in perpetually pending orgasm. Not that any of us knew what orgasm was back then. All we knew, the four of us huddled into that hotbox, was that we finally had our clubhouse. There, among the discarded and co-opted artifacts of the adult world, we could do whatever we wanted.

We could never have articulated what that fort was actually doing for us kids back then, psychologically-speaking. According to various theorists ranging from Freud to Piaget to Eriksen, imaginative play, of which the fort was arguably a physical manifestation, is an important if not evolutionarily significant aspect of personal and social development. Eriksen calls it "the royal road to the understanding of the infantile ego's efforts at synthesis." In *Childhood and Society*, he wrote that kids construct spaces and scenarios full of creative associations, semi-magical if-thens, rules and hypothetical consequences for breaking them (as in, *Step on a crack, break your mother's back*, etc.), all of which come together into what Eriksen calls the "microsphere," a kind of mini-world circumscribed by imagination. As the play continues to unfold, the microsphere acquires more and more complicated terrain, until its geography is so elaborate that it is "endowed with its own sense of reality and mastery," resisting full comprehension or replicability by anyone or anything outside of it.

All of this happens for a reason, Eriksen says. There's a function of play for the child's budding ego, "an attempt to synchronize the bodily and the social processes with the self." Play is what helps us figure out what to do with ourselves in a world we are still getting to know, one we don't fully trust. That summer, we were testing the waters beyond our neighborhood sanctuary to see just how far we could go, literally surrounding ourselves with the very articles that symbolized to us the unknown, the forbidden, the women's pornographic mouths open like ominous entrances to uncharted caves.

And while the significance of play is what happens in the mind, "the child's play begins with and centers on his own body," Eriksen goes on. It happens in the corporeal world.

Consider a baby playing with its toes, what's going on in that baby's brain when it reaches out towards its own body like a foreign object. Eriksen calls this "autocosmic play," beginning before we even notice it as a play. There's a brilliance to the term autocosmic, with its implication of a self-made, reflexive cosmos, an interior universe full of interconnected constellations and uncharted galaxies that point inward, but by some baffling feat of psychological engineering seem to be outside of us, apart from us.

A side of me thinks that if all of this is true, then everything about that construction zone assumes more significance. For example, it wasn't important what was in the briefcase, but what we imagined might be in the briefcase. And come to think of it, why didn't we just build the fort on top of the ground (out of the same cardboard, metal scraps, etc.) instead of under the ground, subterranean, out of view? The element of excavation seems meaningful in hindsight, figuring out how far down we could go (or Lee and Tim could dig) before butting up against the ends of possibility, or in our case, the hard strata of the Mojave Desert. Eriksen says that kids construct microspheres with whatever tools are available from their physical and cultural surroundings. We went as far as we could with Dad's shovel, some cardboard and wood, a briefcase of porn, and the idea of the frontier. Before long, the dark fort, the mottled, empty briefcase, the ominous light of the empty lot, became part of a world we could no longer see, but could only see *through*, a strange mutating lens. Going out there was like falling into a kind of "group-think"—the way people in cults do when there's not enough information coming in from outside to put their beliefs into perspective. It's so gradual you don't see it happening. The anything-goes mentality of the fort was becoming our new reality, to reflect what we understood to be the unsteady rule of law beyond the walls of our childhood, out there in large, sparkling Las Vegas, a world of adults where people were killed in knife-fights and women took off their clothes and children disappeared.

By the end of that summer, Lee and I had spent so much time with the neighborhood kids—especially Teresa and Tim—that the boundaries of our fort had bled beyond the construction zone to the perimeter of the neighborhood itself. It no longer seemed strange that every week another *Have you seen me?* poster was plastered to the telephone poles, or that my second-grade teacher, Mrs. Montoya, watched her Chihuahua blow away in a windstorm, never to be seen again. On our few winding streets, circumscribed by the eerie clearing and, beyond that, the sharp mountains, our make-believe games and imagined scenarios appeared to any ordinary passerby—especially adults—as a harmless bunch of kids on bikes and rollerskates. But to us, we were racing through cities plagued by monsters and bad guys, traipsing through dangerous, tiger-ridden jungles. We were always somehow in battle, fighting the evil forces and winning victoriously. We were taking charge.

One of the worst things we did in this vein was to tell Lindsay that we could finally fix her compulsive laughing. Lindsay was the tag-along in our group, a nerdy, frizzy-haired, freckle-faced girl with glasses and a pronounced chuckle-snort, who lived three houses down from us on the right. Her mom was my Girl Scout troop leader, a position she might only have assumed so her daughter could have some friends. But we all thought Lindsay was weird. She was the girl our moms made us invite to our birthday parties every year. During scout meetings, when Lindsay's mom pricked her freckled arm with the insulin needle, some of us would peek around the corner, watch Lindsay take it with stoic, vacant eyes.

Seeing that was weird, too, because in any other circumstance, Lindsay was always laughing—and not a natural childhood laugh, where the giggle peaks then smoothly decrescendos, you resume control over your facial muscles, and everything goes back to normal. This was different; her laugh was psyched-out, a hungry hyena cackle, nothing graceful in it, nothing girl-like. It sounded desperate and frantic, the sonic equivalent of an invisible hand reaching out from her chest, grasping and flailing, fingers waving and clawing at the air. It was chilling. But it was also something the rest of us kids could make endless fun of, and we did. And Lindsay—probably understanding intuitively that she didn't have the social capital to leverage a counter-critique—was a good sport when we made fun of her, laughing at her own laugh, which would only make her laugh harder until her face registered a real pain around the eyes and mouth as if to signal that things were not okay but there was nothing she could do to defend against it. None of us understood that maybe her loony laugh was itself a defense.

How painful it was for her to laugh that way makes me feel doubly bad about what we did to her. It happened one afternoon when Teresa, Tim, Lee, and I were taking a day off from the fort and riding our bikes around the neighborhood. We stopped on a sidewalk to perch or rest. Someone told a joke that probably wasn't even very funny, and Lindsay started cackling loudly and uncontrollably. Long after everyone stopped laughing, Lindsay was still at it, couldn't keep her shoulders from buckling up to her ears and her mandibles from yacking open and shut. We all stared on, her face contorting into an expression of horror—not at herself, but at what was coming from inside of her, and surely at the frightening sight of us slack-faced kids witnessing her lose it, the muscles around her eyes going taut and her freckle-lipped mouth open, almost crying now instead of laughing, her chest heaving in what sounded like sobs. The cackle went on this way, tears streaming down her cheeks, and then hiccups began and all of us gaped, unsure what to do, not wanting to touch her.

It took the better part of five minutes for Lindsay, nearing hyperventilation, to finally stop laughing. One of us asked, "Are you okay?"

Lindsay looked down at the ground, wiping tears from her eyes. "I'm okay. I just wish I didn't laugh so hard," she said, still catching her breath. "It *hurts*."

It was a moment of truth. Vulnerability bared and stark as the sun-bleached animal bones we tripped over in the desert.

"I just wish I could control it," Lindsay went on. We all looked at one another. She had said a word that struck a nerve none of us knew we had in us. And that was all it took, a momentarily visible crevice in Lindsay's good-natured armor, for the rest of us to slip right in. It was either me or my brother who made up the story—maybe to comfort her at first, or maybe because deep down we knew her admission of helplessness opened up a chance for the rest of us to be cruel in the way only kids can be, in a completely unconscious way. We told her, in utterly convincing straight-face, that we had heard of a secret Anti-Laughing Potion that she should try, and that if she were up for it—you know, brave enough—we could whip her up a batch to see if that might banish the hyena cackle once and for all.

It was amazing how quickly she agreed, as if she had been waiting for something like this to come along, as if just wanting to believe it could make it true.

Consider Eriksen's position that "Often the microsphere seduces the child into an unguarded expression of dangerous themes and attitudes which arouse anxiety and lead to sudden play disruption." He states that it is perfectly normal for a child to try and "take possession of things in order to test them." But he goes on to say that danger can arise when kids are denied the ongoing supervision and guidance to ensure that "the forms of play continue to be productive routes to learning." When that happens, "the child will turn against himself all his urge to discriminate and to manipulate. He will over-manipulate himself, he will develop a precocious conscience." He will try "to repossess the environment and to gain power by stubborn and minute control."

Were we turning against ourselves? Why had we jumped so quickly at the chance to fix Lindsay's problem? We knew that most of our laughing potion story was a lie, that we had no control over Lindsay's compulsion, or over anything else. And yet we also imagined that there was the possibility, in our made-up world, that this might actually have some consequence. Our promise of a potion became a test of sorts. *How much control did we really have?*

At the time, we didn't realize we could have killed her. After the laughing incident, my brother and I scurried home, rummaged a jumbo-sized 7-11 Slurpee cup from the kitchen cabinet and slammed it squarely on the counter. Spelunking through the under-sink cupboards, we found the Comet and dish soap, and from the bathroom, some bottles of shampoo and conditioner, lining everything up on the kitchen counter alongside the carton of milk from the refrigerator (with the new kid's face), some orange juice for taste, various peppers from the pantry, maybe some cinnamon. Once mixed, the official Anti-Laughing Potion was a gloppy, yellow-brown muck with enough toxicity in a single drop to send a test mouse to its maker. If *this* couldn't stop her from laughing, nothing could.

We took it to her that afternoon, balancing it in the Slurpee cup through the street, down the cul-de-sac, and to the sidewalk in front of Teresa and Tim's house, all of us reconvening with a very nervous-looking Lindsay. She looked down at the amber potion, trepidation radiating from her freckled cheeks.

"Will this work?" she asked. Lee and I, along with Tim and Teresa, fiercely nodded yes.

And so Lindsay tipped the plastic cup to her mouth, took a pained sip, the visible part of her upper face imploding, her eyes probably stinging as if shot through with lightning, the soft skin of her forehead seizing up, and all of us looking on, barely breathing, hearts skittering like a pack of rats. And then slowly, slowly, she removed the cup from her mouth, her lips pursed in a kind of trying-not-to-puke expression, her eyes trained on the ground between us all, not yet willing to look up, probably wondering with some honest-to-goodness part of herself whether this might work, her deep-down hope not allowing her to disengage.

It was too late for any of us to feel bad for her. I could almost hear Lee and Teresa and Tim thinking the same thing:

She's going to snap. This is the moment she finally tells us all to screw off, that she doesn't need us or the stupid Anti-Laughing Potion or our mysterious briefcase or pity birthday party invites, when she throws the gunky contents of the Slurpee cup straight into our terrible faces, Tim with his horsy teeth, Teresa's eyes as big as hippos, Lee and I with our goofy grins of mischief.

But what happened next was even more disturbing than any of us could have imagined. Instead of bursting into projectile vomit, instead of raging towards us arms thrashing and knocking us over to scrape our knees on the neighborhood asphalt, Lindsay did the worst thing she could possibly do.

She took another gulp.

We were afraid for the few days she didn't come out of her house that we had killed her, that Lindsay lay feverish in bed, teetering on the edge. We were afraid we had *disappeared* her, that maybe it was others like us that were the cause of all the missing kid faces cropping up each week on the telephone poles and milk cartons, the billboards heading out towards Henderson. But finally Lindsay came out of her house, her frizzy red hair pulled into pigtails and the same freckle-face we recognized from before. We spotted her from down the street and ambled our bikes over to her slowly, afraid to approach her, to see that maybe close-up her skin was as ruddy orange as the potion, simmering from the inside. But when we perched our bikes on the curb and stared at her in silence, our eyes searching for any sign of decay, she just said "Hey guys," like nothing had ever happened, like we hadn't almost sent her to her grave. "Wanna ride bikes?"

Who knows, after all, what Lindsay had experienced behind that closed door, what reason she might have given her mother for puking the better part of three days. She never mentioned any of it, never told us anything about what happened, and we never asked. And while Lindsay's hyena cackle never went away, none of us ever again made fun of it. Her emergence from behind the door was a kind of release for us all. Lindsay could laugh as much as she pleased, and we could move forward knowing we didn't kill her. But there was something more to that emergence, too. I believe that during those days she remained secluded inside her house, the rest of us came by slow gradations to realize that our potion scheme had been borne not from childish meanness, but a deep sense that Lindsay's laugh represented a kind of vulnerability that we all felt, one we had stumbled upon for the first time in our lives that very summer. It was as if the sun had seared a small opening into our childhood oblivion to let in a new, fetid scent. It was the first indication that, despite the fairytales and happy-endings we had been taught to expect, real life was full of things we could not control, could not explain. People were vanishing without a trace. *Kids*. Maybe they were just like us, with bikes and rollerskates, selling Girl Scout cookies on Saturdays. And if they were just like us, what thin barricades kept us from vanishing too? It did not have to be said aloud for us to know that Lindsay's laugh didn't belong in the world we found ourselves in. That tinny, ineffective defense didn't fit with the sense of peculiarity and danger we felt, a world beginning to scare the joy out of us. Maybe, by fixing Lindsay's laugh, we could fix the vulnerability that had wormed its way in, and make sense of a world we did not yet understand. But by doing so, we had become a part of the thing we feared. We were the ones making the caves we disappeared into. We were the ones exploiting those women on our walls. We were becoming the source of our own laughter or reticence.

One weekend that summer, my mother and father took me and Lee to see the old mines in the desert outside the city. We drove for a long time on the two-lane highway, Vegas disappearing behind us over the stark horizon. Finally we pulled off on a dirt road, stopping the Cherokee in a clearing. Looking around, I saw only cacti and dirt, no mines, no trace of silver. I wondered, how in the world did the miners find silver all the way out in this desolation? How could they see what was underground? My dad insisted we get out, start rooting around, look harder at the rock faces. The four of us shuffled through the dirt towards the big rocks, the sun blazing down on our foreheads.

Dad said there was a whole cave system right below our feet, dangerous to explore for all its unpredictable passageways and drop-offs. He said that one minute you could be walking, and the next minute you're falling.

My eyes set on an opening in the rock face, an entrance to one of the old mines. I leaned my head into the dank interior, breathing in the cool, mineral smell of subterranean dirt. "Hello?" I bellowed, listening to my voice echo. Then Lee started up too, both of us saying "Hello? Hello?" giddy at how our own voices seemed to greet us from somewhere else deep within the concealed, byzantine depths of the mine. We were face to face with the craggy entrance to the unknown. What had we been so afraid of?

"Hello? Hello?" we called again and again, our own voices traveling through the caves' dark threads to pick up strange, new traces of calcite, gypsum rock, and dank vapor before winding their way back to us. ❦

Kristin Kostick is a poetry and nonfiction writer currently working on a collection of essays called *You Not You* about the advantages of self deception. She is also a medical anthropologist researching bioethics and health policy at Baylor College of Medicine in Houston. Learn more at kristinkostick.com.

THE NATION OF APHASIA

Xiao Yue (Shelly) Shan

when a writer goes missing in china
we take the red and gold paper emblems
that display the character for luck
off of our doors and paste them
over our mouths. and we go back to
the old books to learn again
what we've learned for millennia,
that you can command armies or
recompose history or traverse
from xian to changsha to mount lu
or buy a dozen eggs and none of it
will mean that your life is a promise
your country makes to you.
hong kong is a dewdrop glittering
in mid-january. we close our eyes
to take its temperature, trying to find
just the right word. the rain
only a sweet-tasting silhouette against
the gleaming skyline. late-day light
spreads a white sheet over the windows
and no one can see in. no one can see out.
still, no one ever thinks this is the day

someone will knock on the door
asking you to identify your husband
by his handwriting. how is it that
we have made a culture out of
paying a heavy price. wearing out stones
with water. chasing the sun across
the eastern front with our poems
closing in behind us like lost birds.
the gardens we do not tend. the paper
boats we do not try in the yangtze.
imagine your life is the thing
that is trapped on the tip of your tongue,
the word that is almost realized,
but you can't quite think of.

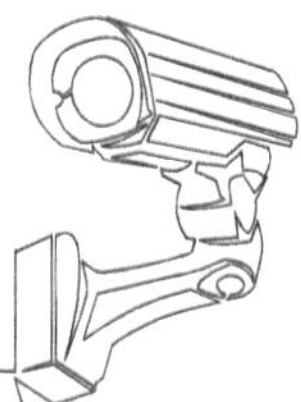

If you're in need of something to write about, I suggest you take a trip to China.

Xiao Yue (Shelly) Shan

New Millennium
Award for Poetry

the nation of aphasia by Xiao Yue Shan

Xiao Yue (Shelly) Shan is a poet and essayist born in Dongying, China and residing in Tokyo, Japan. Her first chapbook, *How Often I Have Chosen Love*, is forthcoming by way of Frontier Poetry. Shelly haunts the internet at shellyshan.com.

This is Shan's first literary award.

LIKE MY FATHER

Seth Simons

I made my first million in oil.
I made my second million in real estate
and my third in a different sort of real estate.
My fourth million I made on red; my fifth,
on black. My sixth million was the product
of some ingenuity involving the Sochi Olympics
and an ill-traveled stretch of coastal highway.
For my seventh through 40th millions I elected
to branch out, building a robust portfolio deeply
concentrated in robotics, artificial intelligence and
spaceflight. I had this notion that the future was
in space, but also computers; the market rapidly
bore out my prognostications. Millions 41 through
399 I made running guns for a warlord of the sobriquet
Hammerhead, "H" to his friends, who had quite
the temper and ultimately wound up in banking.
I'm afraid millions 400 through 450 are classified,
though I will say I'm proud of the work we did
and the work our successors continue to do.
By million 700 I'd really gotten the hang of things.
I had half of Washington in my pocket, the other
in litigation and the patent to a pioneering new
painkiller. I was on magazine covers; my name
graced the marble wings of museums and universities;

I met the president. He told me, “Sergei, you’ve saved us.
Where once was darkness now a small light flickers,
orange in color and muted in character, a paper lantern
gliding almost high enough that it vanishes into the velvet
sky, laden by the gentle weight of human goodness.”
I could’ve taken him then and there. I could’ve
bashed his pretty head with the very medal
he gave me, could’ve socked the spot below
his jaw where it all hinges. Instead I said,
“Thank you, sir, it’s quite an honor,” and flew
my little spaceship to the only quiet place left.

The best

writing advice I have ever received, at least as it pertains to poetry, is to enter a work not with the mindset that I am writing a poem but that I am saying what I think. Obviously this requires me to think things worth saying and really just makes everything more difficult. Fortunately the second best advice I have ever received is to take a break whenever a break feels called for. Walk around, chase a pigeon, roll around in some mud, run on home for a snack. These are all tried and true methods of not thinking too hard, which I generally find to be the most productive thinking of all. It is necessary to qualify all of this with the fact that I don't know anything and fail constantly.

Happy writing!

Seth Simons

New Millennium

Award for Poetry

Like My Father by Seth Simons

Seth Simons is a writer and entertainment journalist based in the Bay Area. His poems have appeared in Rattle, Fugue, Red Wheelbarrow, Breakwater Review, Conduit, Rivet and the McNeese Review.

Subscribe to Seth's newsletter at sethsimons.substack.com and follow him on Twitter @sasimons.

EMBER

Alyson Hagy

SHE FOUND IT WHEN SHE OPENED THE STOVE. It resembled the desiccated carcass of a bird, some tragic dove that had made its way down her lonely, unused chimney. But when she touched it, it moved.

Or perhaps it pulsed. Anyhow, a thin *throb* of color appeared near its center. So she leaned and touched it again, certain it was a scroll of forgotten ash. She was an indifferent housekeeper. It would be just like her to leave behind a modicum of filth.

The thing glowed once more, almost willfully. It didn't seem to produce heat. Just light. Or a prickling somewhat reminiscent of light. The asymmetries it displayed were not familiar. So, despite the faint odor of roasting beets, she closed the stove and went on to other things.

What other things? Money. Fresh garden asparagus. Unpunctuated text messages from her nephews. She had only been trying to straighten up the house. A house she didn't even like.

The stove was the kind that burned wood chopped by stealthy locals. She used it only in winter. Because she was between the yawing moments in life that require true courage, it was late at night before she selected a dramatic bathrobe and returned to the stove.

The glow, what there was of it, had become shivery and sobbing. Not dependent upon her at all. The thing appeared to be recovering from some kind of exertion she had not been allowed to witness. A faint, uncomfortable clawing instigated itself at the roots of her eyelashes. Had she seen a single tongue of flame or only imagined the licking? It suddenly became impossible to leave the stove. She kept vigil for hours. She offered a saucer of water. She planned the shopping for agreed-upon meals. When the cream of morning clotted itself against the window shades, she closed the stove. But not before she touched the thing again. *Palm to heart,* she recited in nervous preparation. It was important: *Palm to heart.*

She tried to go on, with limited success. There was an entire day spent with her head inside the dark stove, singing. There was the trembling offer of a folded, handwritten note.

In the end, she filled the stove with splintered logs and unread newspaper and struck the guardian match. She left the room without a glance. *No burn,* she said to herself, sullied and falsely proud. *It never hurt me. I haven't changed.* Where, finally, was the viper's sting? •

My mentor George Garrett enjoyed reminding me that the only rule about writing is there are no rules. He was right. There are many winding paths toward becoming a writer. You don't need to go to school to become a writer. You don't have to take classes.

You just have to practice...a lot. Stubbornness and perseverance are more important than raw talent. But if there are no rules, there is one thing we all must do: Read like crazy. There's no substitute for it. Read what you love, even if it's fabulously trashy. I cut my teeth on comics and mysteries and historical romances. And I still read them now. But you should also explore. Try genres and forms and cultures that might surprise you. Don't ever get too comfortable. And take big risks—even if it's only in your journal.

Alyson Hagy

NEW MILLENNIUM
AWARD FOR FLASH FICTION

Ember by Alyson Hagy

Alyson Hagy is the author of eight works of fiction, including the forthcoming novel *Scribe* (Graywolf Press). Her flash fiction has most recently been published in *INCH* and *Kenyon Review* (online). Hagy lives in Laramie, Wyoming.

mw

HOW TO WRITE A LOVE LETTER

Eleanor Bluestein

Obtain a box of stationery. Stationery is an actual object; it is different from a digital replica of fancy paper or a digital greeting card. You recognize fine stationery by its subtle watermark. Consult Google Images if you don't know what a watermark is. Whatever you do, don't buy blue or pink; buy white or ecru or, if you must, the very palest shade of green or lavender. Buy the entire box, or if sold as single sheets, buy at least twenty-five. Quantity matters.

Buy a pen. A pen is different from a stylus. You will use the point of the pen to write on the stationery. When you press down, the pen will leave a dark ink mark on the paper. Acceptable ink colors are dark blue, black, or deep brown. Keep in mind that brown may have unpleasant connotations, but that's up to you.

Place the sheet of stationery on a flat surface. You cannot hold stationery in the palm of your hand while you form the

New Millennium Writings, Issue 28, 2019

letters of the alphabet. Note: You are not tapping out letters; you are using the point of the pen to draw the circles and posts that build them. Do not expect the letters to appear without your hand creating each one. Forget about autocomplete. You are responsible for entire words.

To help you understand the instructions through examples, we will use the Jane Doe of the current zeitgeist—the most popular girl's name of the last generation—as the sample love letter's recipient. The name that tops the list is Melania.

To begin your letter, you could try one of the following combinations of words or something similar. *Dear Melania; My Dear Melania; Dearest Melania; My Beloved Melania*. Please note: If the recipient of your letter is not named Melania, substitute the name of the person you are writing to.

It is customary when writing a love letter to write a line or two, then crumple the paper and throw it on the floor and begin again. Keep a waste basket handy beside you. Miss the basket at least half the time, so that rough spheres of crumpled stationery land in the basket's vicinity but not inside it. To produce an authentic love letter, you must fling away at least twenty false starts. This is the reason you were instructed to buy an entire box or twenty-five sheets. After you crumple and discard your efforts a few times, pace around the room before you begin again. Once or twice at a minimum, toss a crumpled missile against a wall or window to demonstrate frustration with your inability to uncover the perfect expression of your affection. Other gestures of irritation are also advantageous. For example: *My Dear Melania*. Crumple. Drop on floor. *Dearest Melania*. Crumple. Throw into waste basket. *My Beloved Melania*. Crumple. Kick the cat. *Most beloved Melania*. Put fist through wall.

Write whole words, not acronyms. You will not, for example, write *DILLIGAS* when you want to say: *Do I look like I give a shit.* Although you probably will not use that acronym in a love letter, it makes the point.

Think in terms of four or more complete sentences. If the muscles in your hand start to ache from the unfamiliar activity, take a break. Ice your hand or spread and close the fingers of your writing hand like a fan. Repeat eight times. Then back to work.

Do not use emojis. No skulls, cats with heart eyes, or guns. You are not writing a picture book. Use your words.

Here are some useful words to insert in your sentences: *cherish; worship; adore; money; power; beauty; greatest; best; immigrant; combover; I; me; you; mine; prenuptial, pussy.*

Do not begin the first sentence with: *I am writing to tell you...* That is so LOL. You are better than that. Simply launch into the sentiments you wish to convey. For example: *I am the greatest and you are Miss Universe.* That's a promising beginning. Still crumple, toss, and start again. *I have wealth, power, and a combover to offer you.* Crumple, toss, start again. *I can't wait to grope your pussy.* Crumple, toss, bang forehead on desk.

Keep at it until you have formulated a straightforward, strong, and confident message. Here is an example:

Dearest Melania,

I am the greatest. You are a beauty. I have a combover. You have a pussy. I will have my lawyers deliver the prenup. You will sign. I have wealth and power and you are an immigrant. You will worship me.

Note: If you do not possess wealth, power and a combover, assess your strengths and cite those instead of the ones in the sample letter. For example:

> *Beloved Kaylie,*
>
> *I am a barista. You like soy lattes. I have an electric scooter. You have a pussy. Etc.*

To conclude your letter, write the following:

> *Adoringly,*
>
> *Your name*

Don't write "your name," write your name. (Please do not use the comments box to ask what that means. If you can't figure it out, unsubscribe.)

Lastly, fold the letter and insert it into an envelope. Now you are on familiar ground. Place the envelope in the drone and tap your beloved's locale code in the address box.

Press Send.

It has been my pleasure to instruct you. Next week's instruction will be: How To Walk a Real Dog. Sneak preview: As the name of our example dog, we will use the most popular AI-dog's name for the previous two decades: Mueller. ❧

In no particular order, this is some of what helps me as a writer: a peer writing group that meets regularly and provides honest critique; reading great writers—past and present; keeping an eye out for the humor in things; occasionally blowing bucks on a pricey workshop; and in successive drafts, trying my best to figure out what I'm really writing about and inching those themes up to consciousness.

Eleanor Bluestein

New Millennium

Award for Flash Fiction

How To Write a Love Letter

Eleanor Bluestein lives in Southern California. She is the author of *Tea and Other Ayama Na Tales*, a collection of linked stories inspired by travels in Southeast Asia. She is completing a novel *Slumming*, and a short story collection *Louder than Words*.

THE LANGUAGE OF RIVERS

Patrick Dawson

THE INDIANS OF THE DESERT HAD A NAME FOR THE RIVER. It translated roughly as *Mother of Time.* They believed the river's great rocks caused the water to speak, to sing. They had faith in the river's voice and its secrets. In the language of rivers, they knew, there are many words for silence.

Marty's hair is cut short and stubby, deep black the color of coal. She has kept it short since the funerals, though she doesn't like it that way. It is a kind of talisman, a symbolic mourning band. A public acknowledgment of loss. Or maybe a form of penance. Though she felt little emotion about their passing. Passing, that was the term everyone used. As though they had been just passing through life like you'd drive through a town on your way to somewhere else.

New Millennium Writings, Issue 28, 2019

Late afternoon. She sits beneath the shadow of the house. In the only place that is even passingly cool. The swift river is just beyond the pasture land, its waters rushing steadily, refusing to yield to the desert, the surface animated by great rocks. But it offers no chill, no relief from heat. Marty's sheer tank top spirals from one shoulder. It barely covers her. She contemplates sitting here naked in the heat, letting the hot wind play on her bare flanks, her belly, down her legs. The house is empty, after all.

It is almost four. Marty should go pick up little William. She would have to change first into something that wouldn't be talked about. She is a young girl in a desert town. The place is weary; its ways, even its air, indolent in the sun. Streets hushed like a churchyard. On the main street, working men gather in front of a bar at the end of the day. The bar is called Billy's Sundown and has been there forever. Even in the shadowy corners, it pulses with the desert heat long after the sun goes down. So the ranch hands spread themselves across the benches outside. They press cold beer bottles against their foreheads and speak in short bursts. Marty knows the men talk about her after she passes.

The strangers among them, mostly young men with careless eyes, and off by themselves. There is a row of flag decals on the window where they lean against the wall and a hand-lettered sign faded like an old stamp that says "NO Loitering."

At first, the boy had been one of them, one of the strangers.

She first saw him sitting on a khaki duffel bag, head down, thumb extended pointing up the highway. The pitched heat at midday was white, impregnable. The sun lay on him like rust. There was one cottonwood nearby casting a mockery of shade. From the backseat of the Marins' car, he appeared to her like a statue of dust. They were driving slow. The desert air blew in the car windows and lifted her hair from her face. It was six miles to town. A single gliding vulture, its wings in a shallow V, circled above, expectant.

Mr. Marin did not stop.

"Don't know why they come here. Not enough work for our own."

He said this as though giving a speech, to no one and everyone. His native drawl slipped into a stutter when he was agitated. Wordless, staring at the road shimmering with heat far ahead, his wife didn't bother to agree.

He shook his head. "You never know what they're running from."

Marty made sure they weren't watching when she looked back through the dust at him. *The boy may be a stranger here,* she thought, *but he knew enough to avoid the shade where the rattlesnakes gathered during the day to escape the high desert heat.* Her only other thought: *He was probably just passing through.*

Marty lived in a spare room on the ranch that years before had been storage for hay and feed. It held the earthy smell of deserted barns. She tried to hold back her displeasure when Mrs. Marin first showed it to her.

"My husband doesn't really like having people living with us in the big house. But if you want, now and then we don't mind if you come up for meals."

The woman looked away when she said this, uneasy with her lie. Marty sensed the first whiff of trouble. Thin, vaporous, it was gone in a moment. A ragged snap of wind from a coming storm.

"It's okay. I can make it work." Marty's voice held just a touch of doubt and impatience. She would not make it too easy for the woman.

That January, shivering in her small cabin outside Boulder, she had pondered the ad. *A nanny with some background in teaching.* That week the cold around the cabin seemed to enter her, pressing against her bones like metal. She checked in the newspaper at the library and it was twenty degrees warmer in New Mexico. That's all it took. Life turns on a weather report.

Marty had never taken care of kids. Her brothers were all older. But a few teaching courses in college had been enough to satisfy the Marins. She would take care of the boy and start some basic lessons. They offered her board and $50 a week. It was less than she wanted but it was almost spring, and warmer, and anything seemed possible.

The room had an aluminium shower wedged in the corner. Marty hung a plastic sheet across it, which kept the water from the floor but offered little privacy. Sometimes she didn't mind that, bathing in a fantasy of someone watching her soap the day's heat and sweat from her bare skin. The room is sparsely fitted out with an iron bed, straight-backed wooden chair, and the artifacts of a life still vague. There is a paper lantern, somewhat-Oriental, throwing a thinned-out square of light on the floor. Her alarm clock that emits a constant hum. A box of paperback books is pushed to the end of the bed. Objects that exhale solitude.

At night she drank beer from a can and listened to radio stations from cities distant enough to stoke illusions about the lives of people there. She had grown up in a small city in a small state. The past year she had been with a man-boy named Luke for a time. He was 20 and worked on an oil rig. When the well and the work expired, he was gone. She got a letter a month later, a single page of motel notepad with scrawl almost too hard to read, emotions too feeble to care about.

"You look lost."

The drawl, wide and flat, glides out of the haze of voices. *Oklahoma,* she thinks.

Her answer is directed to the amber drink in her glass.

"No way, cowboy. This is my bar."

Marty runs a wet finger slowly across the bar forming an arrow that points to the door. She is not certain of the meaning.

"I work out on the Darwin ranch…since last month…first time I've been in here."

Silent, she listens to the pauses pile up like dust against the side of a house. Yeah, Oklahoma. She's almost certain.

Marty waits a beat, then one more, sure of what he will say next.

"What do you do?"

Right on cue, she marvels. Her eyes plumb the depths of her drink. She speaks without looking.

"I'm an expert on human frailty."

His lips are now pursed, eyes thoughtful, the words weighed just long enough.

"Given what I've seen, the town should keep you pretty busy."

She waits another beat then catches his gaze in the mirror. Oklahoma is waiting too, she knows this. His face is shadowed with some audacity she doesn't recognize. It seems devoted to something worthy. She is aware of his hands which have a steady, heedless kind of grace.

"And you've come to take me away from all this, I suppose."

"No, I'm stuck here too."

It is a small insight, but there is a kind of casual honesty. Also, he has left the stool between them empty, which she likes. It is a measure of patience in short supply on Saturday nights here.

She shrugs. Her voice is playful. "Then you better sit down."

There is a long moment before she recognizes something in his presence, something familiar. It curls her mouth in a half smile. It is the dusty boy from the road.

Her question is part demand.

"Do you have a…"

He fills her pause.

"Taylor."

"First or last?"

"First."

"So we're on a first name basis already?" She is teasing, probing at his defenses.

"Well, *tempus fugit* and all that." He says this like a shrug.

Now she wonders if this may be a mistake, considers how fast even the bold ones lose the advantage. All that potential brought down by a cliché.

"Saw that on a greeting card did you, Cowboy Taylor?"

Watching his eyes, she waits for the hurtful expression to fill them. That stupid, doleful-boy look, the *I thought you were nice* look. His eyes are languid though, resting on her.

"No, it's from Virgil originally. It was in a book that I really liked."

Perhaps because he says it so quietly, she feels he is not showing off.

"Is it? So we're playing name-dropping the classics?"

The fat bartender, the one who filled in some Saturdays, is walking up the bar wiping the surface, inviting himself into their midst. His crew cut, trimmed razor-short, makes his face featureless. The words tumble from a mouth that barely moves.

"You folks doing okay? Need something?"

"No, we're good. Taylor here was just telling me all about Virgil."

His expression spreads from disinterest to confusion.

"You mean that half-wit boy at the filling station?"

"No, this one is from out of town."

He nods, his face once again empty. She gives him the smile that says all is fine for now, then turns back.

"What's your guess, Taylor...you think Virgil at the gas station knows much Latin?"

"Maybe not."

"Well, let's not shortchange his potential." Marty is pushing the ice cubes down into her drink. "On the other hand, I've been here awhile and I doubt I've heard a word of Latin. The place is dead, not the languages."

She is watching his hands again. They are relaxed, resting on the bar. He seems unscathed by her insolence.

"That could be the result of that human frailty you mentioned." He takes a slow sip from his beer bottle. "You know the *tempus fugit* thing is mostly misunderstood. What most people think of—if they know it at all—is *time flies*."

"And you're going to tell me that's all wrong."

"Well, they say it's not so much a cliché. It's actually more subtle, different meaning entirely. More like...time is lost and will never come again."

She knows he is enjoying this, doing it for her. Card tricks with a dead language. There's boldness in her eyes. She has left her uncertainty behind.

"Well, that Virgil was nothing if not subtle. Unlike our Virgil here..."

Like a chorus, they both say it.

"...down at the filling station."

Moonlight gilds the surface of the water. The cool plateau of river plays against the heat and the quiet. Against the dark. It is an invitation. He is a few steps ahead of her on the path. The darkness falls open to receive them. Marty wonders if she ought to be afraid. She imagines herself one of the desert animals out there right now, foraging in the night. Like them, she is prey raising its head to sniff the air for danger. Unlike them, she feels a need to be careless.

At the water, they are joined for a moment. The sound of unseen creatures nearby. All around the clatter of the night. She recalls the moist corners of his mouth at the bar, the jagged force of his gaze. In a kind of joyousness, she leans into him.

His voice holds a lesser drawl now, as if intimacy is softening the edges.

"Your skin is so warm."

"Everything is warm here," she whispers, "you'll learn that."

All at once, Marty feels there are things she needs to reveal. She wants to hold his face in her hands and blurt out secrets. Confessions, desires. Her only allegiance is to this moment. She knows it is not love. It is simpler. Something between imagination and revelation. It is a rich thrill.

She sees a thin yellow cross against his skin. She feels her own nakedness, how good it is. Then the cool river water is around them, the current a kind of shared skin. Beneath the surface, Marty opens her eyes and he is there framed by the halo of light above. His hand barely touching her. The river is a dark tunnel, its water passes above and below, gliding along her like a caress. She wants nothing more.

Afterwards in the quiet, Marty wills him not to speak. Wishing for only stillness. Just the music of his breathing and the night. There is a storm in the distance, flashes of light behind the mountains. The sign of heaven glittering in the dark.

Taylor comes once, maybe twice a week. He parks the old borrowed pickup at the main road and walks to her so the Marins don't know. Some nights they creep out of her room laughing silently like children and share his sleeping bag by the river. There is always the river, and they are often still awake as the desert light rises, comes to glisten on its surface.

He is looking at the sky.

"Have you noticed the people here don't so much complain about the heat as immortalize it."

"I felt a little immortal a while ago." Marty murmurs this shamelessly, her hand clasped around his thigh, pulling him to her. Her desire is still raw like a wound.

There is a minute or two before he speaks again.

"My granddad was an outlaw." He says this indifferently, as though reading an entry from the encyclopedia. Her longing will have to wait.

"And mine was Wyatt Earp."

"No, he was, truly."

It is embarrassing to her how she loves the way he says *truly*. She knows he is that earnest. When he sleeps, there is something admirable in his face. She often watches for the slight tremors of his dreams, as though it was where the truth of him lay.

"It was right around 1900...West Texas. He said it wasn't really a bad life, I mean a bad person's life. Claimed we all have a bit of larceny in us, just some people act on it more than others. And he never shot anybody. Said as long as you didn't shoot anyone or steal horses, the Texas Rangers would leave you alone."

The light has now begun to gather around them.

"And how did this tale of the Old West turn out?"

"Apparently, he was involved in some kind of mishap, mistaken for someone else. And in this mishap, someone got shot. That's when the Rangers started after him. He decided to retire just across the border in Oklahoma, took to farming."

Her mouth is on his throat, not really a kiss. She wants it to be intimate, maybe even chaste. Her question is a murmur.

"What about your parents?"

He shifts slightly, leaving a small space between them. For the first time she senses a wariness, as if some cruelty trailed after him.

"My father was a different kind of crook. He sold insurance to small farmers scratching out a living...a hundred acres of top land, a handful of underweight cattle. You listen to him, the talk was pure Texas. Like his people had been at the Alamo and he owned ten thousand acres."

Something lifeless is now in his voice. Marty remains still beside him.

"The insurance was always more than they needed, more than they could afford. You know that expression, all hat and no cattle? Well, that was him. Oh, and he drank...professionally."

His words sound depleted, tired.

"That's why we got out."

He says nothing of his mother. Marty can sense a darkness there, the void.

"Who was 'we'?

"My little brother and me. We went to live with my granddad."

She feels his hand on the inside of her knee, only a faint touch, weightless. The sweep of a cat's tail. An intimacy restored. Yet something now suggests she may enter only when she has consent.

"So your daddy was a crook and granddad was an outlaw..."

She says this as much to the sky as to him.

"Yeah, I'm thinking maybe I should run for office."

He remained quiet then.

Nights come, then days. The summer air is porous. The heat hard like iron. During these weeks, Marty has taught herself not to anticipate. She is not sick with love. There is only a sweet tenderness, and sometimes the lash of desire. Somehow she knows she will pass just the days with Taylor, not the years. He will be a sentence only half-written.

Early morning. The scrim of night slowly drawn back. The river is flat-gray and sullen in the faint light. They are dressing when the gun slips from his bag, the leather bag Taylor always brings along. That he is never without. It gleams in what is left of the moonlight. She knows this is nothing strange, not in this part of the country. Still, she feels something then, something in the way he places the gun back in the bag. In the way he says nothing. A thing suddenly brittle between them. As if they are no longer co-conspirators.

Walking back to the house, he is quiet. Marty cannot shake a single image from her mind. The old man, his shock of pure white hair, his pale Stetson riding one knee and two small boys, rapt, listening to the stories. Hearing him tell the outlaw tales, the psalms of his country. The way of life that cannot be reversed.

"I came here looking for them." He says this in a measured way, laid out evenly like cards being dealt. They are standing together just beyond the barns. He is looking at the big house.

The words are oddly austere. Yet she has the feeling of being lost in a whirlwind of things shifting, as in the moment before driving into a rainstorm. It is then Marty thinks of how much she has shared about the Marins. About the house, the money.

"For them, for the Marins? Why?"

A long silence follows.

"My brother did some work around here. Did some work for them, and for people they knew."

His words are simple enough, non-threatening. The barest of facts. *My brother worked around here for them.* Yet she can feel their sullen force, that they are seeded with menace. That there is more he will not say.

What has been missing.

"Until he didn't work for them." This last has a sharp edge.

"Taylor, you're confusing me...it's even scaring me a bit."

There is a spasm of flight from a tree above them. Birds suddenly alight in the dawn, birds of prey. Unseen, the day has opened. His face is spoiled with tension, dark circles stretch below his eyes.

"Rock me on the water, soothe me with your mercy..." He says this as though thinking out loud.

"What?"

"It's something my grandfather used to say to us. Something between a prayer and a warning. It was a sign that something tough was up ahead. My brother said it just before he hung up last time we spoke. He was laughing, but I don't think he meant it as a joke."

She is silent after this, waiting.

"I know he was around here until a few months ago. He used to call every couple of weeks. And then the calls just stopped."

"Maybe he just took off for California or Mexico…like an adventure. Maybe there was a girl."

"He would have told me."

"Do you want me to ask the Marins?"

"Be better if you didn't, I think."

Faced with a stab of something absolute in this, her assent is wordless. And Marty recognizes something else, something beyond anger. A stubborn force, but something holy in it too. What was honest and calm in him, now threaded with a grave intention. She wanted more time alone with him. Time to order all this…before what? To say what?

Some conclusion, unsparing, unknown, gathers around her. They stand saying nothing then. The sky is featureless, as if the heat had scoured all the life from it. A mirror of the land. The big house is not yet awake.

Friday, almost evening, and Marty is waiting for the Marins to return. She thinks Taylor may be at Moran's later. She is making William's dinner while he plays just outside the porch door. The boy is beautiful, the kind of informal, temporal beauty that will endure only a short time. A wistful child murmuring a song of his own making.

The Marins have gone to town. *To meet the others.* At least that was how it sounded. Marty had heard them talking in the hallway before they left. A slipstream of angry, strident whispers. It was clear Mrs. Marin didn't want them to go. When she finally agreed, her voice held something ruinous in it. Bitterness, perhaps directed at herself. The acrid taint of surrender.

"I want a tree house."

William is stacking lettered blocks into a structure that seems incapable of standing.

"Are you sure? A tree house can be kind of scary and high up." Marty says this through the screen above the sink. "Suppose we make a fort instead?"

Marty knew they would never let him have a tree house. The boy didn't seem deterred.

"No, a tree house. So I can hide from the bad man."

She only half-heard this, barely registering the imagined demons of a five-year-old. Then after a few seconds, Marty thought to reassure him.

"There are no bad men here."

"I saw them talking to Daddy."

"Are you sure…where did you see them?"

"In the town. I was in the car. The bad man was outside talking to Daddy and then he hit him. And he fell down."

She again weighs the realm of imagination in a lonely little boy. But there is something earnest in his voice.

"What did your Daddy tell you about it?"

"He said not to cry. And that only boys should know about this, not to tell Mama."

He is holding back tears. The only time she has seen him anything but content with his world.

It is after ten. William is asleep and she can hear ordinary sounds, as if everything were the same. The windows are open, a night wind lashes at the house. Marty knows something is wrong. Mrs. Marin would have phoned. She wants to call Taylor but has no phone number. She wants to elude the fear rising like water around her.

In the morning, the sky is scoured to a whitish blue. Twin fence lines mark the edges of the highway. Driving north to south, the deputy is first aware of the smell of gasoline. It lingers in the air, metallic. Then he sees the vultures circling ahead. The landscape is stark, prehistoric. The desert here has taken everything. Except the car. Thirty yards from the road it lies flipped over. A dead insect scorched black on all sides. The Marins' bodies have burned inside. So much so, there will be no real remains to be examined. Just human ash, like something sacrificial.

The deputy approaches with his handkerchief held to his face. New to the job, his hands are trembling. He is a young man, his face unlined by trouble and he is here in the presence of death, in a field of dust. Stumbling on the uneven ground, his boots kick the loose, dry earth ahead of him. The dirt will bury all the spent shell casings. The vultures circle slowly, patient as priests.

In the first days of Taylor's absence, Marty clings to the faith he is still somewhere near. That he will show up late at night, sleeping bag thrown over a shoulder. Until she knows better. It was just for a time, two saplings bent against one another by the wind. What else had she imagined?

In the river, there are now torrents of water, foamy and yellow from the sandy banks. The hard rains of autumn have pushed it almost beyond its banks. The cascading river that will give up the body. Give up its dead. The body has been submerged a long time, trapped beneath the great rocks. Distorted, its face smoothed of features like a balloon, it looks like no one; it will be impossible to identify. Had it not spent so much time in the water, someone might have recognized the features. Like a younger version of that boy that used to work the Darwin ranch.

Marty walks in the early mornings before the heat rises. The light is silver. Little William will go to relatives soon and then she will leave. For some things there is no explanation.

When she thinks of Taylor, about the last time she had seen him, he is shirtless. Standing in the river near the bank, surrounded by the large stones polished smooth by the current. His back is wiry, browned by weeks of work in the sun. The work done by strangers. His jeans are covered with the dry dust of summer to the knees where the river water had dyed them the color of night. He is motionless like the stones. She can imagine walking the long path to the river and standing in the water close enough to feel the heat from his skin. She would stand very still while the water bears their reflection in its cool surface. In dreams anything is possible. Especially with strangers.

There is the sound of the days passing. It carries everything along with it. At night she lies in her room, the bed turned to the window and the river breeze. Marty is twenty-four. She is a girl in a desert town. She knows the freedom of loneliness, the soft weight of longing.

In the river, the angry torrents have subsided, its peace restored. In a few hours the desert heat will begin again. The 7th Cavalry will be home next year. The dead President will be young forever. ❧

A critical lesson

I carry with me from a career in journalism is that stories told through the prism of character carry a special resonance. The most powerful narrative - war, an earthquake, even the toppling of that which we thought was steady and permanent - is just a procession of details until invested with nuance or texture by character. "The Language of Rivers" started with the image of a girl - not yet a woman - against a landscape of the desert. Simple enough. But Marty dragged me along with her through the months of 1966. Her character, and the things she learned from the other characters, allowed it to become a story. It is the implication of life, the complexity of its experience that the character grants us, sometimes without us even recognizing it.

Patrick Dawson

New Millennium
Award for Fiction

The Language of Rivers

Patrick Dawson spent nearly three decades as a journalist, most of it as an award-winning national and international correspondent for NBC News, CNN, and ABC. He is currently at work on a collection of short fiction and a novel. He lives in London and New York.

This is Patrick's first literary award and his first short story to appear in print.

mw

SINCE

Patricia Sammon

April, 1866   The 20th or 21st

Husband,

Three days of snow have imposed a heavy silence on the town. To this I say, *good.* It is difficult enough for me to compose my thoughts to you without my having to hear mule teams racketing along the planked road.

You recognize the red-ruled paper I sliced from your ledger. I will enclose two more sheets so you can write back to me. I doubt the Denver jail makes gifts of stationery to its inmates.

It is thanks to the snowstorm that I learned you are alive. All this time I have been sorrowing and you have been just two days' ride away. My informant was a rough-looking sort of a man. He banged at the door and asked if he'd been lucky enough to come upon a brothel in the middle of a blizzard. I told him I was the Widow Maddox and that I run a clean boarding house. (Yes, Husband, I now have a boarding house.

New Millennium Writings, Issue 28, 2019

Hush. I cannot begin this letter to you from all different points at once.) The man remarked on my name. He said he'd arrested a man named Maddox a few years ago. I told him that while it was true that I did not know the particulars of my husband's death, you had been possessed of a fine moral character and you were no criminal. Then I told him to get his horse off my front porch and make his way to the saloon, which he would find more to his liking. He asked if your name was Joe Maddox. I will tell you, Joseph, my limbs gave way. I had to sit on the blanket chest and struggle for breath. He asked if you were a gold miner. My hopeful heart flapped like a caught goose, but I resisted. There are hundreds of gold miners in these territories. He told me he was a bounty hunter and he recalled the Maddox case because you were no ordinary criminal. He said that all you did was poke fun at how some poor fool in the mining camp was making his coffee. Oh, Husband, you have ever been such a tease. When the insulted man lunged at you, you knocked the gun away but it discharged, killing someone's horse. Now you are reading this letter, fretting over your ledger paper and interrupting me about how it is we have a boarding house, and wondering why I wasn't offering this man a free supper for bringing me news that you are alive. But you know me. I like to get a clear sense of what's what. I demanded to know why the law would arrest a man for knocking away a gun. He pointed up the staircase (Yes, our house has a staircase now) He asked if there mightn't be a few sporting ladies up there. I blocked his path and insisted he tell me why you were locked up for self-defense. Up close, the man was not so ferocious-looking. There were beads of ice in his mustache and they swung in a silly sort of way as he spoke. He told me that if you'd just paid the one-dollar fine the judge charged you for the act of provocation, you would still be a free man. But being a hothead, you stormed out of the courtroom and a bounty hunter had to be called. I asked if he'd captured you on the mountain slope above town, panning for gold. He said no, you must have been in a high, holy fury because when he surprised you were well north of here, by Camp Collins.

Do not be disheartened, Husband. There's a smart chance your sentence is almost fully served. And now you are holding this very sheet of paper in your hands and you are reading the words of someone who is not, after all, a widow. It will be some time before the roads clear, but I will come to visit you after the next thaw. I've never seen such deep snow. Yesterday I looked out from my upstairs window and what did I see poking up from a great snow bank—the tips of branches where I knew no tree stood. Annie helped me reach the place. You don't know who Annie is but never mind. Just read about a tree that was not a tree. Annie and I had to use swimming motions to scoop and kick a path. What we came upon was a deer, perfectly alive, buried in the deep white. Only the tips of his antlers reached beyond the surface. His eyes were black and large. I put a rope around his neck. He followed me back through the snowy corridor to the house. Did he think I was leading him to safety? I grabbed hold of the antlers and wrenched his neck and he crumpled to the ground, foaming at his nostrils. We need food, but it did not seem a fair or proper hunt. More like a crime that I did not mean to commit. I used my knife to slice his neck and drain the blood into a bucket. For a time, that bucket held the only color in the world.

In all the times that the mail courier has stopped here to buy a meal of corn bread and cup of stew before continuing on his way, I never had the thought he would one day be carrying a letter from me to you. The snow will delay his arrival here, so I will add to this letter when I can. Right now I must attend to the front hall, which is puddled by heaps of wet scarves and socks. When you return here, you can set an example for these boarders as to what good grooming and *care of appearance* mean. Remember, five years ago, when our wagon train finally reached this territory? Remember the general amazement when you opened your wooden crate and took out a neatly folded, black linen jacket? As if you'd known all along you were going to meet a woman on the westward trip and you'd be in need of a wedding coat.

I hear one of the boarders coming upstairs. I will ask him the date and add that to the beginning of this letter.

2 days later

The last time I waved goodbye to you, your new sluice box and tin pans were making a merry noise as your mule trotted along beside you up the mountain slope. When you did not return at the new moon as planned, I tramped uphill to find out if you were sick or hurt. I went first to the big mining camp. The men said they hadn't seen you. If they were gentlemen, they would have told me about the fight and your stormy exit. But they are not, and they did not.

I made my way to your stretch of river and fully expected to see you there, kneeling by the water's edge, swiveling the tin plate. You—in the grips of gold fever, forgetful of your wife in town or your need for coffee, beans, lard. Then I looked for you crouched among the boulders, working your pick ax, reading the grooves like some old scholar. But I couldn't even find your sluice box and pans and rocker irons. Not even your tent, though I fingered the holes in the dirt where you had staked it down. Husband, you often teased me about my genteel upbringing but let me tell you, frontier life has made me sturdy. I marched further up river to the next claim. The man kneeling there by the water's edge was red-headed and stout, but still I had the idea that he would become you, turning at the sound of my voice. I hallooed at him for a while before he heard me above the roar of the river. I asked about you and he said *Git!* The mule beside his own tent looked just like yours but then, all mules look identical. I asked if there had been any trouble with bandits. He took his rifle and fired once into the air. I asked if that meant yes or no. He leveled his rifle so that it was pointed at me. I turned and left. Let me tell you, I was not afraid of that scoundrel. I was so angry I was like an image in a wavy mirror. He had nothing to aim at.

Yes, Husband, there is now a mirror in the front hallway. And I have an upstairs room from which I can look out over the fields. You will find many more changes when you return. There are about fifteen new homes in Clear Creek. The supply goods store has doubled in size.

I had none of the blood pudding I made the other evening, but the men all had extra helpings.

How lovely it has been just to tell you a little about how things are with me.

Your loving wife.

Last week of May, mud everywhere

Husband, perhaps I am not so very sturdy. I had to fight back tears when the mail wagon from Denver brought no letter from you. I know you have barely had time to read my letter, let alone begin an account of the past three years since we saw each other. Another courier will soon pass back through here on his way into Denver. I want to have a letter to put in his care, so I will take up this pencil whenever a quiet moment presents itself.

I had not realized, until I learned that you are alive, how neatly your death had fit itself to the corners of all these rooms that I sweep and mop, day after day. Your stillness was my steady work. Now, like a wakened breeze, you have tossed all the curtains and rattled the door hinges. I am glad, of course, but I do not mind telling you I am flustered at the thought of seeing you. I find I must grip the stair railing even when I am carrying nothing.

The day after I told the marshal that I had searched your claim and could not find you, the bodies of twelve miners were washed into town, cruelly delivered by the roaring snowmelt. Finding that you were not among the drowned brought me no relief. The following month a Mrs. Smith, mother of five here in Clear Creek, wondering at her husband's failure to return home for a month's supplies, walked up to his claim and found the poor man's body, flyblown in a gulch, a bullet in his back, his tent ransacked.

Drowned or murdered, the two means of your death propped themselves upright against one another, and I knew I was a widow.

I have my own news to convey but I know the only news you want to hear right now is what became of your claim.

The answer is, I asked the marshal's help to sell it. Do not be vexed. You must realize I had to find a way to survive. I sold the claim for $148 and gave the marshal $1, which he did not want to accept but his wife is sick and I insisted. I did not hide the $147 in that particular place in the house where your pouch of gold dust and your scale are buried. Not even Annie knows the hiding place. Joseph, when you return, you can give up prospecting and use the gold you buried in the house to buy some cattle or sheep. Yes, the snows get deep here and they can close in on grazing animals but you, on a horse, with a dog, would make quick work of the round-up.

5 days later

You can be sure that the cash from the sale of the claim felt alive and kicking as I walked over to a group of newly arrived wagons. I struck up a conversation with some of the women. Yes, plain, quiet Me can be a church bell if I need to be. When I made it obvious that I was a respectable sort, I asked if the men could gather round. I addressed my inquiry to a kindly looking man. Joseph, do stop interrupting me! I admit that I enjoy the sense that you are reading over my shoulder as I write, but you must not rush me. You want to know why I would carry a fortune in a dress pocket when I was going to meet strangers. I'll just say that it seemed yet more foolhardy to leave a fortune unguarded in the house. And the reason I knew the man was kindly was because he was holding his young boy on his hip and tickling him. I told the assembly that I needed some construction done on my house. I wanted it greatly enlarged, with a second story.

I wanted the walls to be made of proper brick with framed windows and I wanted the inside to be canvassed and papered. The father holding his boy asked if he might know how I would pay. No, Husband, I did not show the money. Just read! I said the marshal could vouch that I had $147 in cash. The men were happy for the work. Mining equipment is always more expensive than anyone expects.

Annie helps me run the place. She does not want me calling her an Indian. She says she is a Shoshone. Can you imagine such cheekiness? She is about as ladylike as a wild cat. At first I was put off by her ignorance. She was actually afraid to tread on the stairs, never having seen any before. But I have come to put great store in her ferocity. My boarders would sooner have her drop them out the second-story window (she is no longer afraid of the stairs) than have her catch them trying to steal anything. Last month before the big snow, she and I were scrubbing laundry alongside the stream. She noticed some young boys getting too close to the butter box that was cooling there in the ripples. She threw pebbles at the lads. I suppose that wasn't a friendly thing to do, but it had taken me a long time to churn and set that butter. I do not know what her real name is, so I gave her the name of the little sister I had for a time. It is pleasant to hear the name flit about the hallways of this house whenever I need help.

Your loving wife.

Mid-June

Husband,

By now you know a mail courier stopped by the Denver jail and asked if inmate Maddox was receiving his letters and the jailor said you are. To which the courier said, "Then please pass along word that Mrs. Maddox awaits a reply." Did the jailor call you hen-pecked? To that I say, *good.* I do not care if you are being teased. It was teasing that got you into this bad luck. Send me word in your own hand that you fare well enough. Our marshal here in Clear Creek has reason to go to Denver soon, and he will check on your wellbeing himself. I long to abandon this boarding house and go with him, but of course I cannot travel alone with the marshal, especially now as he is widowed.

Last night when the house was filled with snoring, I went downstairs to the dirt floor where your gold is hidden. I just wanted to touch what you had touched and smooth over again what you had smoothed over. I am building my courage to write to you of everything that has happened. No, I am not being courted by some young fool. No, I am not in debt and tempted by your cache. Here is one interesting fact for you. It was rumors of gold that caused Julius Caesar to leave the known world and set off across the ocean to invade the island of Britain. Are you surprised I know such a thing? As surprised as you are to learn that there is a plank street in Clear Creek and a wild Shoshone woman helping me wash clothes and fry up bacon and cabbage for our boarders?

A year ago, one of my boarders confessed he'd be unable to pay the month's rent. I told him that before he cleared out he had to give me something of value to cover the debt. I suggested the calf-skin boots he was wearing but he pretended not to understand. He said he owned several books and he opened his valise so I could see my options. One book was a treatise on temperance and I said I was already well familiar with that topic as my deceased husband had felt favorably about the cause. Another was a published lecture on how to dig irrigation ditches for desert farming. The next wasn't a book at all but a photograph of Ulysses S. Grant in military uniform, standing by a tent. I told the man I'd grown up in a big home with a fine library and didn't he have a good reading book—something by Cooper or Poe. He said he had only one other book: *The History of the Roman Conquest of Britain.*

Annie is calling that she is ready for help with the laundry. I do not go into the various rooms to collect dirty clothes. If a boarder wants his shirts and socks washed, he needs to leave them in a basket by the back step on Monday morning. I will go down now and see how many of the men remembered such a simple instruction. They will grumble this evening at dinner that I failed to remind them. Lord, that Annie can scream. If the mail carrier comes tomorrow, you will get this letter without a proper ending but you will not care.

Mid-Summer

The first time I read *The History of the Roman Conquest of Britain,* I had to keep my knife at hand in order to slice apart the pages. But now I have read it often enough that the pages are well-thumbed and smudged. Before Julius Caesar set off for Britain he asked some merchants who traded in the northern realms to tell him about the habits of the wild men of Britain. He was informed that the Celts do not fear disease or death. "Do they fear anything?" the scribes record Julius Caesar asking. And came this answer: "Only one thing. They fear that the sky could fall down upon them." I find that so strange, Joseph. Not afraid of suffering or death. Only the heavy hand of the air above.

Last night my history reading carried me once more to a famous surprise attack on the Celts. Just to set you straight, this is 100 years after Julius Caesar. The emperor of Rome is now Claudius and his general in Britain is assembling his forces at the banks of a river, in full view of the Celts on the other side. The general has his men staking their tents, digging ramparts, and setting up large cooking fires. I put myself in the place of the Celts and I pretend I do not know what is about to happen. I look across the river and I wonder what to think about all this activity. *Are they building a town? Do they mean to stay?* Meanwhile, Husband, a special force of soldiers with the Roman army has snuck away from the great commotion. In full armor, at a much wider stretch of the river, they swim across. The Celts had not known that men in armor could swim, let alone that they could swim so well that they would choose a wide stretch of river just for the element of surprise. Husband, the surprise was terrible. The special force did not begin by attacking the Celtic warriors. They attacked the horses and mules, slashing tendons and muscles so that there would be no animals to pull the dreaded Celtic chariots. Each time I read this, I think of the bellowing animals, the smell of blood. When the bounty hunter pounced on you, near Camp Collins, what became of your mule? If you were in such a fury about the one-dollar fine, why did you not just come home? I would have hidden you well. Then you could have slipped away from the town under cover of night and set up somewhere you could not be surprised by the law or bandits or floods.

The historian of the Roman invasion is one Reverend Welland-Smythe. He is of the opinion that the surprise attack took place at the River Medway because he found Roman coins with the image of Emperor Claudius buried not far away. But the Rev. W-S says we will never know for sure. He makes ample use of the phrase *lost to the mists of time*. I wonder if the Medway is a slow-moving, peaceful river like the South Platte, or a raging torrent such as Clear Creek. I asked a Cornish miner who boarded here for several weeks about the River Medway, but I could not understand his answer. His words were English but so strangely knotted together they held no sense.

October 30th, 1866

Husband,

I heartily repent of my impatience. The marshal returned with word that you are among those inmates who recently enlisted with the militia in order to hurry the completion of your sentence. Well bully for you, but now you are pressed into dangerous work, fighting Indians who only want to fend off invaders.

Last week there was word that Indians were going to raid Clear Creek. Annie refused to join us as we barricaded ourselves in the saloon. She said if the raiders were Shoshone, they would not bother her. And if they were Utes, she'd kill them herself.

I forget that these Indians are not just one large group. The different tribes wage war against one another. Reverend W-S is of the opinion that the armored soldiers who swam across the wide stretch of the River Medway were not Romans but Celts, disloyal to their own people. I had not even allowed for that possibility. Perhaps it was a traitorous friend who directed the bounty hunter to your hiding place near Camp Collins.

The rumor of an Indian raid began because an old couple, traveling at dusk, spotted shapes along the mountain rim. Who can imagine what they actually saw—a bear and her cubs, some Shoshone slinking deeper into the western mountains. I find myself siding with the Celts more and more.

The mail courier dreaded telling me he had no letter for me, but I told him you were off fighting Indians and would soon be home, carrying my packet of letters with you. As he ate his stew, I pestered him for news of the world. He said there was fever in Boston and Philadelphia, and earlier this year a ship traveling from Britain sank, taking hundreds of lives. Certainly troubles are evenly distributed the world over.

Four days later

The boarder across the hall coughs a good deal and I can feel the draft from his open window, flowing like an invisible river beneath my door, pooling at my feet. Mr. Johnson cannot possibly be his true name. He claims to be a New Yorker, but I suspect him of being a Slav or even a Turk. He has odd, foreign habits such as bobbing his head as he serves himself a bowl of soup, and smiling when no one has uttered a remark that is either funny or pleasant. But he pays promptly and happens to smoke a tobacco that puts me in mind of you. I still think of you each day, Joseph Maddox, as these pages make manifest.

Mid-November

Husband,

I am myself a house of strangers. Inside one room, I pace back and forth, thinking of you. In another room, I make lists of the hundred things that must be ordered if this place is to be kept running. My own memories belong to someone else. They are the big old boots lined up at my front door. I close my eyes and see my baby sister in her cradle. But I must be imagining that scene. I was only four years old when she died. I try to remember my father's library. I can feel my hands on the wooden steps of the ladder, propped against my father's great bookcase. Was I really allowed to go up and down that ladder, holding books? Unlikely, both for my sake and for the sake of the books. If I take my time I can see the tasseled lamp, the patterned carpet, but then my father in his casket, looking like someone else's father. Mother, begging in the street, looking like someone else's mother.

Tell me, Joseph, what was the first thing you said to me? Ha! I knew you would say you can't recall. I knew you'd just straighten your collar and tuck in your shirt and say, *Such foolery*. Here is the answer. The evening you first spoke to me, the wagon train stopped only a few days out of St. Louis. As I gathered fuel for the cooking fires, I was telling the little children stories about *Ivanhoe* or maybe the headless horseman. You teased me about how gingerly I picked up the buffalo chips. Then you asked me what kind of work a storyteller was going to do out in the territories.

I never properly thanked you for asking that question. It let me see myself as others saw me—a scrawny young woman who would be a burden if all she knew how to do was tell a few stories. Then and there I started teaching the children their sums and letters so I could win myself a place at the cooking fires. I wish Annie would let me give her a few lessons. She refuses to learn how to read or write and says our people will be gone one day and her people will return to their old ways. Who is to say? Certainly the Romans do not prevail in England today.

Last night my reading carried Claudius's general beyond the victory at the Medway. Emperor Claudius himself must make the long journey and preside over the final conquest. The general waits, busies himself building a timber road and also a bridge at the River Thames. When the emperor arrives he brings war elephants with him. What must the Celts have thought of such giants? I once saw a picture of an elephant. It was on a circus poster. When that circus was about to come to town, we were still a well-to-do family. But by the time the circus had arrived, there was not a nickel for admission. Father was bankrupt, then sick, then dead.

Joseph, I am unable to sleep, no matter my exhaustion. I sit at the noon of night, using up fine tallow candles, waiting for your return.

The Rev. W-S says that the Celtic chieftain who died of his wounds at Medway had a twin brother who survived the battle and traveled off into the western mountains. I do not know what became of that brother. Perhaps there is another volume to the history book. Perhaps no one knows. That is more likely.

Now that the pencil's lead is worn so soft that it outraces my scribbling thoughts, I will tell you what I must tell you. Let me begin by remarking on the inanities uttered by well-meaning people who hope to offer consolation when a baby dies. *A better place*, the Reverend of Clear Creek said. *The Lord called her home*, said the mothers. I wish you had been able to return from your claim at the new moon as you had planned. I would have told you I was bearing a child. When you returned again for supplies you could have met our newborn babe. But now, since I know a little of the history of you and me, I am grateful you were spared the heart-stab of losing her.

I named our daughter Josie, for you. She kept me in my right mind as your death settled into fact. She was a year old and taking her first steps when the sickness struck. Would it be any help to know for bottom fact that it was diphtheria? What I do know is that the fiercest armies attack unseen, inside stagnant air. I lit buckets of tar to rid the air of pestilence. It did no good. Her eyes were open as I sang to her but her lips blued and her gaze clouded as if she were at a great distance though she was right in my arms.

I like the phrase *a vale of tears*. It is a good expression. It matches perfectly what it means to be alive. Josie's burial took place April 15, 1864. I put her in a white dress and the coffin—which had been a box with a shipment of rifles—I bedded with the striped calico of my old dress.

Two days later

Annie knows all the words that have to do with laundry and cooking , and those are enough to include words for *river* and *wooden boards* and *mud* and *grass* so, the other day, as the two of us were boiling up beans and salting some mutton, I told her the story of you and me traveling west and of our adventure crossing the river. First I helped her see the twenty wagons moving out from St. Louis. I told her I couldn't remember the name of that first river we encountered. It was deep and had an uncertain bed, muddy and thick with grasses. I told her it would not have been suitable for cleaning clothes. I explained that our head driver determined we must take apart each wagon, haul the boards and axles and wheels and bundled canvas across the water and then reassemble the wagons on the other side. I let her see you there: tall, shirtless, standing in your dark trousers. I told her you climbed up onto the back of one of the horses and guided it as it swam safely across. Then you returned to get on another horse. Seeing your example, I hopped up on one of the horses. You said it was a foolish thing to do in a dress, but you had to admit I could ride. On the far bank you watched me wring river water from the dress and you said, "You would make somebody a good wife." And you laughed when I said, "You asking?" I don't know that you ever did ask, but you were smiling when you put on your good-looking jacket and the Reverend placed your hand over mine. Did I speak vows? I must have. Then we set off for Clear Creek to minister to your gold fever. I don't know how much of the story Annie was able to understand. Perhaps it sounded like a succession of strange facts about a time that has nothing to do with her. But when I turned to her, she smiled, helping me hold up the largeness of such a beautiful recollection.

Tonight, it will once again be 55 BC. Julius Caesar is setting off across the ocean. He does not yet know about the strong tides that will damage his ships, and I have no way to warn him. He has not yet seen the fierce Celts, their faces stained blue. Next month I will reach the part where Emperor Caligula (Husband, he comes before Claudius) goes to Britain and orders his men to pick up seashells as bounty. Perhaps Caligula was not in his right mind. Or perhaps it was not *seashells* he said but something else and the scribes wrote down lies or errors, or made spelling mistakes.

Your loving wife.

Late Spring, 1867

Husband,

During the past year I wrote several letters to you. I know now that you did not receive them. No matter.

I am dictating this letter to Mr. Johnson, who has promised to faithfully write down my words to you. He is the only person in Clear Creek who has contracted the fever and survived. It kills young and old alike. Last night it claimed my only friend, a woman with long, dark hair. The disease advances by orderly progression beginning with something the doctor calls *Break-Bone ague*. I think Break Bone is a good name. Certainly I am unable to hold a pencil.

Last month the marshal discovered that the person who was held for a time in the Denver jail for provoking a fight has a name that sounds exactly like yours but is spelled differently.

So that is the end of that.

Shortly after learning that you were never in jail, I received a visit from the man who bought your mining claim. He said he had found some shards of bone in the riverbank and feared they were evidence that you had drowned. He presented me a packet containing splintered fragments. They were tangled in a scrap of fabric that might have been wool or blue denim, but could just as easily have been canvas sacking. He expressed his condolences and then left to see his family. The marshal told me the bones look like those of a deer. The cloth is moldered and useless for identification. I buried the packet at Josie's grave. You don't know who Josie is, but that doesn't matter. The guess about deer bones was the marshal's last official act. Four days later he was dead of this fever.

I enjoy the thought of Mr. Joe Madicks sitting in the Denver jail, reading of the details of a stranger's life. Perhaps the letters are not lost to the mists of time. Maybe, upon his release, he brought the packet home with him to Camp Collins. I think of him as married now, with a young daughter to whom he will tell stories about wild, blue men. His eagerness to hold his daughter tight will be the only evidence that I ever lived.

I am glad it was not you who was jailed. A lonely plight, that. And not in keeping with your fine character.

Having had you alive for the past year, I cannot quite shut the door against the thought of you returning here one day with a story for every scar on your body, your eyes lit with a teasing smile. Did you take apart your life and reassemble it elsewhere? Did you travel on alone, forsaking the pouch of gold you buried here? I do not think so. You are not a disloyal person, and you were definitely not one to be heedless of a good supply of gold. Just think of your fury when you were told to pay a simple dollar fine! Ah, but of course that wasn't you. There are more shadows in this room than a single candle and a desk and chair and scribe can account for.

I leave you this farewell. And I leave you a history book that I enjoyed. Mr. Johnson has told me my thoughts are disordered and that I should speak no more but rest. I will do so, but I have insisted he write down what he just said to me, and then that he write down this one last thing.

This history book proved to be a fine sluice box. I rolled it back and forth and caught many sun-flash glimpses of you. ❧

Daily writing sessions usually end abruptly—"Wow, I have to get to work/ I have to pick up the kids"—and the wonderfully dazed, altered state in which I had been immersed vanishes the moment I turn on the car radio and rejoin the outside world. But I've found that if, instead, I move in silence as I head to work or to pick up kids, I can float in the gradual diminution of that altered state and there are often connections and insights that rise to consciousness. Sometimes these insights can be breakthroughs, and more often they are simply good starting points for the next day's writing session. Either way, I scribble them down before I get out of the car. I've come to rely on the small gifts of the 'after-glide.'

Patricia Sammon

New Millennium

Award for Fiction

"Since"

Patricia Sammon was born and raised in Canada and immigrated to the United States when she was 16 years old. She studied history at Cornell University, then completed graduate school at Queen's University in Canada. Sammon has written a novel, many short stories, and is working on a play.

mmw

FALSE MEMORY

Marsh Rose

For almost three decades I have believed in this memory: When I was 40 years old I fell in love with a bush pilot in Alaska. He was rugged and unique and fearless. He thought I was amusing, a genuine California hippie, and he invited me to visit, showed me the sights and sent me home. But blinded by the wonder of him, I pursued him shamelessly. When I went back to see him and found out he had another woman, I was mortified, I was angry, I recovered. Later, when I learned he had died in a plane crash, I was sad. And that was that.

And that, as it turns out, was not what happened.

I've kept a journal since I was 13. They're piled up in boxes along the back wall of my bedroom closet, a vital but unremarkable presence, like my toothbrush or my shoes. Now and then I dip into that collection of notebooks and binders, words on napkins from truck stops or in the margins of maps, but usually the boxes remain closed, sometimes for years.

I knew that somewhere in that running narrative of my life was the brief story of my big romantic tragicomedy, me and the bush pilot. I never talked about it. Making a fool of myself over a man when I was approaching middle age was an embarrassing segue best forgotten. But in a nostalgic mood one frigid December afternoon, when the northern California monsoons were streaming my windows with rain, and even the dog wouldn't venture outside, I decided to relive the full measure of that experience in Alaska. So I fished that journal out of its box, draped a shawl across my shoulders, and curled up on the couch to read.

I was feeling fragile in the spring of 1989. My long-term relationship had ended the previous year and there seemed to be no hope of finding love again. I would say that I would never need a man. However, if pressured I would admit that I wanted one. Wary of the singles scene with its illness and treachery, I remained lonely and alone until I heard of a magazine for women looking for romance. It featured bachelors in Alaska, the place where single men outnumber women by three to one. Meeting someone *in absentia*, from a distance, would be safe and controlled, so I got a copy and there he was: a lanky, shaggy-haired Alaskan version of Crocodile Dundee. As I read my journal I smiled to think of the way I had gasped at the sight of him, standing barefoot on the pontoon of his float plane on a summer day, shirtless, innocently holding a slippery, wet, freshly-caught salmon at the level of his navel.

I wrote to him and he wrote back. There's no copy of that exchange in my journal but I remember being galvanized by his response. He wanted to talk. How my heart pounded when the phone rang and I heard his voice for the first time.

So we began a telephone and letter correspondence. In my journal I wrote about haunting the mailbox for his envelopes filled with photos and stories of life in the harsh bowl of the Alaskan interior. But as I turned the pages in my notebook, the story wasn't evolving as I remembered it. I heard a distant note of alarm and confusion. In my memory I was thrilled with the attention of this Renaissance man, fantasized about an affair with him, dreamed of life in the *last frontier*. So what was this journal entry from a few weeks after our first conversation?

May 20, 1989

He phoned last night at 11:30 p.m. and we didn't hang up until after 1. I cringe to think of his phone bills. I know he's interested in me but I get in my own way. That long, grainy Georgia southern drawl. I wonder if his father voted for Wallace. Hell, he was old enough to vote when Wallace ran in '72. Maybe HE voted for Wallace! And he named one of his daughters Sheena Kay. Not only did he name her Sheena Kay, he calls her Sheena Kay. I mean, at least call her Elizabeth or Mary. The poor girl is going to end up wearing square dance outfits and singing karaoke in a biker bar.

When had I forgotten these doubts about him, this ridicule? I remembered only being swept up in the fantasy of him, blinded by love and oblivious to his indifference. Feeling unsettled by the unexpected tone, I read on.

Four months after our first conversation, Rusty invited me to visit. I thought I remembered my reaction—as ditzy as a schoolgirl and behaving like one, raiding camping supply outfitters and used clothing stores for wear that might be suitable in Alaska. I remember my anticipation on that flight north, certain Rusty was falling in love with me as I was with him. But while my journal indeed told a love story, it wasn't the one I remembered. Two days after I landed in Fairbanks, I sat on his deck in the noonday sun with my journal on my lap and wrote.

August 16, 1989

Alaska has burrowed into my soul. Like an iceberg, its depth is hidden. I felt it when I stood beside the river near his cabin. There was a shift and the landscape itself became sentient. Something darkly feminine seemed alive in the woods, the lumbering clouds overhead, water that appeared to have an intentional rhythm. I suddenly felt I knew what men experience when they fall in love with a beautiful, unattainable woman, those who invite a chase but can never be captured and will never be an ally. I craved her acceptance. The sense of presence dissipated. I decided it was my imagination, my thoughts moved to Rusty standing beside me in his lumberjack gear, all high cheekbones and auburn hair and wide-apart green eyes. But when I turned from the sight of him back to the river, my awareness of her returned, watching me, dispassionate. She's been on the periphery ever since, coming up in dreams, sinking down like an ancient coelacanth.

And sadly, while I am in love, it's not with Rusty. The social, cultural, spiritual, and emotional chasms between us are too vast. I can get lost in his arms, I can thrill to flying with him in his little plane over the Denali Preserve near his home, but lust and adventure will yield to impatience. His right-wing politics clash with my liberal attitudes. If a force consumes me, it isn't Rusty. Alaska. I try to capture her with words and she flings herself against my cage, her hind legs scrabble, dig in, her claws draw blood from my opened palm. Or worse, she pulls in, tucks under, fetal position, silent, eyes like slits. Finally I give up, stalk away, heels down, not caring anymore, damn it. Then when I'm beyond the realm of consciousness, asleep, there she sits at her opened door with her tail twitching. She stretches and saunters out, passes me, languorous, not bothering even to graze my cheek.

Reading my journal, I felt as if I were in the darkroom again with my father, an amateur photographer. He taught me how to develop a black-and-white photo. We would plunge a sheet of exposed paper into a developing solution and swirl it until slowly, amazingly, an image would swim up out of the fluid, at first dim and indistinct and then more and more clear.

August 21, 1989

Last night I jokingly remarked that I was scattered all over his cabin and didn't know how I'd pack up. He said, "Yes, you're scattered all over this cabin. You're on the deck writing, on the riverbank looking into the water. You're with me trying to tear this bed apart and

I don't know how I can watch you pack up and leave. Can you stay awhile longer? Just one more week?"

That passage told a story so dissonant from my memory, for one moment I wondered if I'd made it up, violating my own rule about crucial honesty in my journals. But as I read the words I heard his voice saying them. And my journal brought back from the distant past the way he held my eyes as I prepared to board the flight home. "We're not over yet," he said solemnly. "I'll see you again."

In the following weeks back home, although I never mentioned it in so many words, in my writing I sensed in myself a softening, a change. Qualities that I once found worthy of ridicule about Rusty were now endearing.

October x, 1989

We've spent so much time talking on the phone, I think I'm beginning to develop a Georgia accent. I'll sound like a character from Gone With The Wind, my all-time favorite movie. I like its slow, lazy tone. Rusty carried his phone outside tonight so I could hear the sounds of crashing birch trees as the beavers worked on reinforcing their dam in the river. I was entranced by those small animals with their industry and determination. Rusty says that's what it takes to fit in there, animal and human. I wonder if I could measure up?

He urged me to return, because I loved Alaska and because he felt our relationship had a future. Would I give him a chance? Yes, we were different but it was the heart that mattered. And didn't I want to experience Alaska in the winter? *Christmas in the frozen north is an acquired taste*, he said seductively, *like raw oysters, best licked and swallowed in the company of an experienced friend.* He described that view from his deck, the light on the water and how the deepening autumn was changing the colors in the forest, always reminding me that I was welcome there *in my home and in my arms.* What force had caused me to skew my memory so that I was the supplicant? A pulse began to hammer in my throat.

November 10, 1989

Yesterday I got a hefty package from Rusty. Along with his photos and letter were the help wanted ads from the Anchorage Daily News, the only paper for an area the size of Texas and New England combined, with jobs that might appeal to me circled in red. Maybe he's right. The pay is better in Alaska and I can see myself putting down roots there with Rusty, the very essence of the place, as my guide and mentor. When I think of going back, my blood sings in my veins. My best friend Dana cried on the phone. She said whatever happens, my life will never be the same. Mom and Dad are upset. They refer to Rusty as "that man." When I speak of Alaska, it's a place on the map. It's snow and ice, sun and shadow, wind and the tracks of animals. But in my soul, Alaska is ancient artifacts and incantations, peace and fury.

She lives in me now. And Rusty understands that part of me. It's a part of him too.

I looked up from reading, shook off the images, and took a few deep breaths to slow my heartbeat. My living room swam back into view, my books on their shelves, my dog curled up asleep beside me. If my altered version of this experience had ever fought with this story of what really happened, my false memory won and the truths sunk down below the surface of my awareness. Those truths, now sparked, began to ignite others. They flickered in the back of my mind, not quite within reach. If this much of my memory was awry, what would I learn now?

December 22, 1989

I am home, shaken but safe. Rusty is history. I was in the cabin alone at 10 a.m., dawn was a salmon-pink line on the horizon, Rusty had gone to work and the phone rang. The machine picked up. A woman called him sweetheart, said the homeowners had accepted their offer on the house they were buying together. My blood froze. And there was more. It had been there all along. On a shelf behind the coffee cups, a large paper bag filled with letters. Now with the sound of that phone message still in my ears, I sensed what they were. All bets were off now. All decent behavior. I spilled them onto Rusty's scarred kitchen table. There were dozens and dozens on different stationery with different handwriting. The earliest postmarks were from nine months ago, when he appeared in that magazine. The most recent were mailed last week. I read. Some were casual, some were funny, some read like poetry and others were barely literate, but all were from women who believed they were in a serious relationship with Rusty. The most recent, written on thick cream paper in delicate handwriting, was heart-wrenching. It was from a high school teacher in Oregon. She had quit her job! She was packing! And then he phoned to say he met another woman, a film producer named Susan. My name isn't Susan and I can't work my own camera. My letters were in there too. I felt nauseated. When Rusty called me all these months, half the time he wasn't even in Alaska. He was calling from different towns along the west coast, cruising around meeting women in airports, homes, cafes, and motels. Those gorgeous descriptions of the view from his deck as the seasons changed...were they all fabrications? Was he really in some woman's bed in Seattle while she was in the kitchen making a post-coital snack?

The dog awoke suddenly and looked up at me. I must have made a sound of shock or surprise. I reassured her that I was okay—I probably sounded insincere—and went back to reading.

Each woman got the photographs. Some got the help wanted ads! Each one thought she was the love of his life. One was living in town with her teenage son, expecting to buy a house with Rusty. Her name wasn't Susan either.

> *I was more frightened than angry, and packed with my fingers shaking. Then I bundled up, tucked my jeans into my boots, and slipped and slid and ran to the cabin down the road. Bruce and Allison's, I had met them. I begged a ride back to the airport with a story about a sick relative. Lies were in order. No holds barred. And I didn't leave a farewell note. No confrontation, no accusation, why bother. Just that stack of letters on his table and the light blinking on his answering machine.*

So that was the heart of the true story, the one I had been hiding from myself all these years. I needed a cushion of denial between my psyche and a painful reality. I had been duped in a dangerous game by a narcissist, possibly a sociopath. I don't know why he did it, what pleasure he got from convincing vulnerable women that he was in love with them. I don't know if any of the others had been furious enough to exact revenge. But reading on, I learned that something tragic had happened to one of them. It was in the news of his death, more details I had forgotten. Here in my journal was the clipping from the *Anchorage Daily News*, sent by that neighbor who had found my address among his belongings and thought I should know. April 21, 1990, off the island of Ruby, Alaska, two fatalities, a pilot and one passenger.

> *A witness saw the Maule M-5 suddenly bank left, upend and crash into the Yukon River. FAA records show that the person seated in the pilot's seat had his pilot license revoked in 1988 for operating a civil aircraft under the influence of alcohol. The toxicological report for this*

immediate incident showed that the pilot had a blood alcohol level of .195 percent. The passenger's name is withheld pending notification of next of kin.

I shakily got up to make a cup of tea. In my mind's eye, I was flying with Rusty on that August afternoon, looking down at the panorama of the Kahiltna Glacier 4,000 feet below. Only months after I had fled the cabin on that wintry day, he had been drunk at those controls when he pancaked into 40 feet of frigid water. Fate, blind luck, or perhaps divine intervention had kept me from being the unidentified woman in the passenger seat. In Alaska—a place where personal aircraft are as common as motorcycles in the lower 48 states, where daredevil behavior is the norm, and alcoholism is rampant—flying while intoxicated is not tolerated. Even jokes about it are met with narrow-eyed silence.

And that teacher in Oregon. Were it not for the overheard phone call and the telltale letters, I too might have been picking up the pieces of a shattered life. My journal showed that I thought of her more often than I thought of him in the following weeks, and considered writing to her about the lies and manipulation. But I never did. I'm not sure if I was guarding her vulnerability or my own.

After a few rocky months, my journal never again mentioned me and the pilot. Soon my life in California changed for the better. I met someone to love and never went back to Alaska. Its hold on me shrunk to a well-worn copy of Robert Service's *The Spell of the Yukon*. "There's a land, oh it beckons and beckons."

It was dusk when I closed the pages, wandered back to the closet, and slipped my notebook into its place. For the next few weeks I eyed the row of journals with suspicion, as if they were jack-in-the-boxes waiting to spring another unwelcome surprise. But eventually I made peace with my false memory. We all rewrite the past now and then. Our slanted versions keep us going. Without them we might be stopped in our tracks by foolishness or shallowness or rage. I don't know when the truth about this experience began to craze and fracture in my mind and my false memory took its protective hold. But I believe both stories are true in their own ways. They're both now a part of my living past and my immediate present. ❧

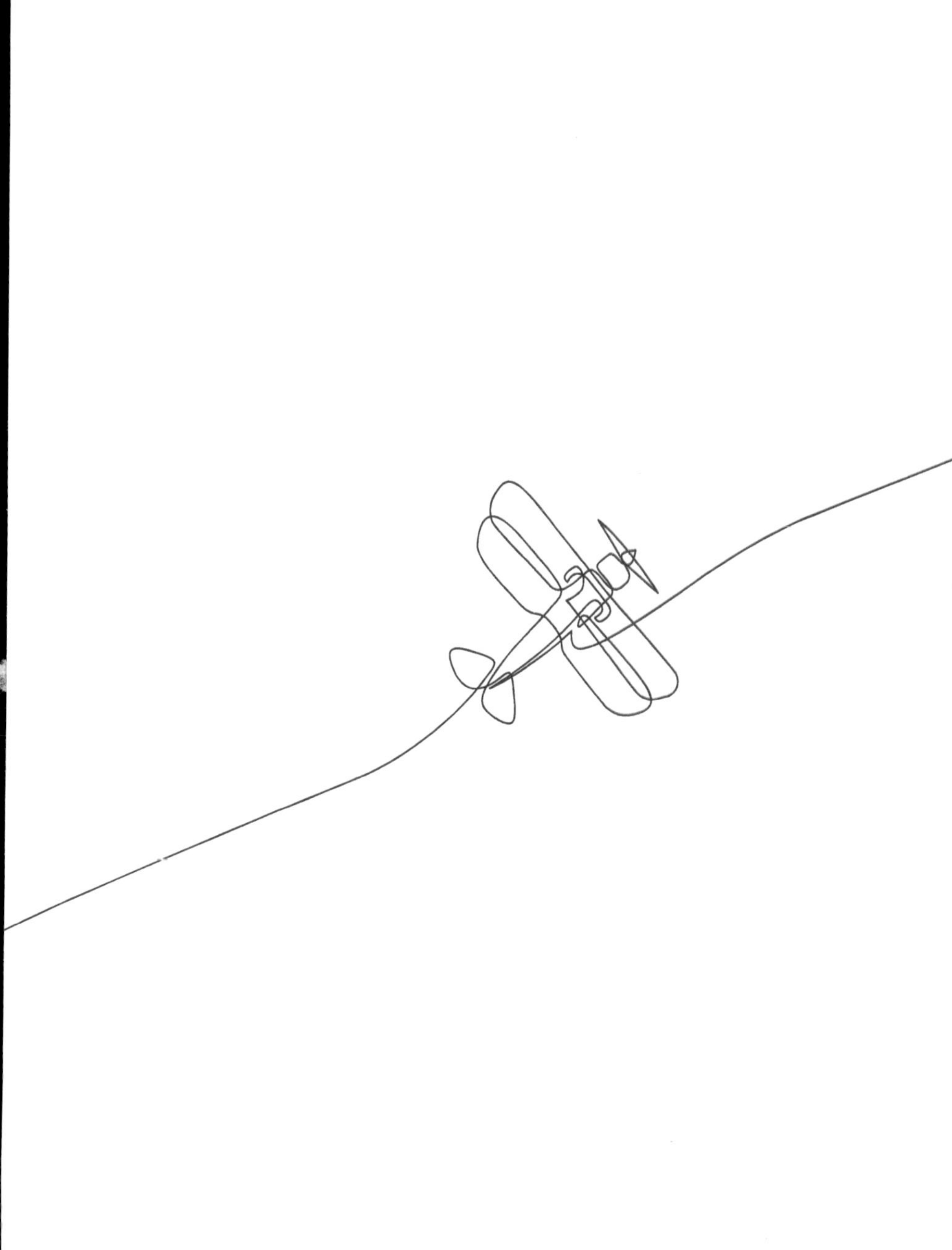

I have a secret.

Every Sunday and Wednesday morning, whether I want to do it or not, I trade at least 1000 words of writing, often in ghastly shape, with my writing partner. Within a few hours she emails back my work with gentle comments, and I return hers. Our commitment is fierce and we apologize for those rare times when something keeps us from our routine. Major surgery, that might get us out of a day's writing. Or sitting in the center seat on a 16-hour flight. We've kept it up for more than 15 years and we've each seen one another through a novel and a memoir and almost countless essays. I would become lazy if I didn't know there was a set of eyes out there waiting for me to fulfill my day's promise. Finding a good writing partner isn't easy. Oh well, finding any sort of partner isn't easy. Let's not go there. But one is out there for you—you meet in a writing group or a workshop, your aunt knows a writer, you see someone writing every day in a coffee shop. Go get a writing partner. I'm serious.

Marsh Rose

New Millennium

Award for Nonfiction

False Memory by Marsh Rose

Marsh Rose is a psychotherapist, freelance writer, and college educator living in northern California. Rose's short stories have appeared in a variety of publications in print and online. Her writing style is narrative nonfiction.

This is Rose's first literary award.

mmw

BLANKING

Kristin Kostick

ON ENTERING HIS STARK, BEIGE-COLORED ROOM, MY dad was introduced to Grandpa Tom as "an old friend." His name didn't seem to ring a bell. Tom had greeted him with a smile like he might greet a business partner. Firm hand shake, steady gaze. Dad said it was like meeting a different person. He seemed kind, his wild white eyebrows looking like something out of a storybook. But something about his grin resembled a meddling vine overtaking the façade of a house you'd grown up in, something you go after with a machete and trash bags.

Grandpa Tom couldn't remember anything from his life, not his profession, not the names of his parents, or even what his kids look like. My dad says the tell-tale sign of his total memory loss was the big smile the first time he visited him in the assisted living facility. Dad hadn't seen him in years, and all of a sudden he gets a call from a half-sister my dad never knew he had, saying that Tom is in the hospital and one of them should probably go and tend to him. Grandpa Tom can remember the names of his kids, but nothing else about them. "*We haven't told him who you are,*" is what the nurse whispered to my dad when he arrived at the facility, as if my father were committing espionage.

Grandpa Tom has something called "wet brain," technically called Wernicke-Korsakoff syndrome, when the neural pathways that deliver memories get zapped after a lifetime of heavy drinking. The condition is caused by a lack of thiamine or B1 in the brain, which heavy drinking prevents your body from fully absorbing. Because he lived alone when the effects finally set in, no one was around to see Grandpa Tom's symptoms worsen, his coordination declining into a staggering, irregular gait, bumping into furniture or knocking over his whiskey glasses in bouts of disrupted motor coordination. No one was around to know if his visual and auditory hallucinations sent him wailing aloud in his living room or slumping deeper into his armchair, pouring another round. No one could see what Tom saw from the inside, his abnormal eye movements and double vision blurring the pictures on the walls, the labels on bottles. No one was around to witness the piecemeal loss of memory until it was already completely gone, until he was checked into the hospital. No one was there to listen with him when the doctors issued the prognosis: *Total recovery extremely unlikely.*

The nurse leaves. My dad and Tom decide to walk the grounds along a meandering path through open grass and trees. The two men don't have to think about where to go—that's why the path is there, my dad realizes. It lets you simply walk and talk, the body a vessel for conversation. Grandpa Tom tells my dad that the people at the clinic treat him "okay," but he doesn't know why they're keeping him there.

"I don't know what these *other* guys are in for," he says. "I'm not getting too close or friendly with them." Dad realizes that Tom thinks he's in some kind of prison. "I haven't done anything wrong," he insists. If they don't let him out by December, Tom says he's walking out. He doesn't realize he arrived on a one-way ticket.

My dad calls me long-distance when he comes back home, astounded that Grandpa Tom really can't remember anything, that the brain can just wipe away memories like fog on a steamed glass. In the photograph he later sends me of the two of them together, smiling into the camera, I think: *Who is this small man, standing next to my father? Why does he look so happy?* In the awkward, distant composition, my father stands over him nearly half a foot taller—a distinction that seems to me symbolic of my father's greater integrity—a strained smile strapped to his bearded face.

Given that I never knew Grandpa Tom, apart from meeting him once or twice as a child, I am not familiar with all the things that he did or said to my Dad throughout the years. The fixer in me wants to know every story, to chronicle the pain inflicted on my father in the same way an accountant wants to mark every error on a spreadsheet in order to arrive at a final, ameliorated total. But a laundry list of offenses will not change the past, nor prove that Grandpa Tom didn't *mean* to spend most of his life making choices that would culminate in the way my dad's voice lodges in his throat just saying the word "dad." All of what I associate with my own father—strength, integrity, generosity, kindness, conscientiousness—are conspicuously absent from virtually every anecdote I have encountered about Grandpa. My impression of Tom as a kind of cowardly, accusatory, anger-displacing, and self-loathing character is cobbled together from a series of brief moments in my life when I have witnessed the effects of these traits on my father, whose face has only a few—but thoroughly memorable number of times resonated with sheer sadness and disappointment in response to Tom's affronts. I never needed to know the details. The unforgettable look on my father's face was enough to convey all.

I'll just say it: Maybe out of protectiveness for my dad, I'm skeptical about Grandpa Tom's *total* loss of memory. I understand the lack of thiamine, the impaired function—I understand what alcohol can do. But I also can't help but recognize how convenient it is for Grandpa Tom to suddenly lose his memory *now*, as he approaches the end of his life, when ordinarily the lonely hours ticking by in the dim light of his living room might represent a justifiable finale to all the years he had wronged himself and wronged his family with selfishness and drunkenness, and when looking around and realizing you have nobody might spark a recognition of culpability so strong that one would wish there were something else to be done, a way to backtrack the years, to pour the drinks back into their caramel-colored bottles and whisk them back to their boozy store shelves, everything speeding up in reverse so that the weight of your guilt and self-disdain as you settle into your worn-out recliner begins to fade faster and faster with the possibility that maybe none of that was real, that entire life you just lived must hold *something* more, cannot be left like that, and everything *must* rest open to revision or you'll go mad with the guilt of squandering it as you did, that there exists a way to go back and do it over, or failing that, to fix it somehow and make it right or like it never even happened at all, surely there must be some undiscovered mechanism among all of the universe's enigmatic machinery, that allows us to reconfigure the past and shape anew the future into something brighter, more beautiful, nearly sparkling with possibility.

How convenient, I think, to go blank when it's time to reclaim your life's earnings and you realize there simply are none. Does he *really* not remember my dad? What about the time he finally left my dad—then only eight years old—to take care of his younger sister and his mom, her multiple sclerosis worsening every day? Does he really not remember all the letters my dad wrote to him over the years, trying to forge a relationship and never receiving anything back other than occasional letters penned in Grandpa Tom's drunken scrawl? Or the time my dad finally brought his son—my older brother—to visit him, to show him that my father had proudly raised a *man*, and my brother and dad had walked into Grandpa Tom's house to find him fire-breathing drunk, totally indifferent at their arrival? That neither?

"I don't know if I want to read it," I remember my dad saying, returning from the mailbox one Christmas with a card from Grandpa Tom in his hands. I was home from grad school, and it was just me and Dad that Christmas. I remember the decorated tree blinking blindly behind his tall frame. Dad paced the room, which I had never seen him do. I remember watching him open the letter with a small but doubtful smile playing on his mouth, and then silently reading the card. He stood there clutching it in his hands, reading for a long time, though I could see from where I sat that there were only a few lines written on the card, and that the handwriting was big and messy.

I distinctly remember, too, how when Dad started to cry, the tears didn't stream down his cheeks but clung instead to the surface of his eyes, the way globs of water stick together in outer space, in zero gravity, the water anchored only to itself. I remember how he had crumpled the card in his strong fist and flung it into the trash, letting the words that Grandpa Tom would never remember writing mingle with the leftover ham bones and pie crusts.

I had never known anyone else who'd lost their memory. My only knowledge of amnesia came from a social anthropology class I used to teach, and whenever we got to the subject of identity, I always showed a documentary to illustrate the idea of identity as *constructed,* something we create for ourselves, not out of thin air but from our cultural and personal experiences, under the influence of the world around us. *Just how much can we construct our identities?* was a question I always posed to the class. The documentary was about a man, aged 35, who "woke up" one summer morning in Coney Island on the F train, having no idea who or where he was. He had a British accent, a backpack containing a pair of swim trunks, a learn-to-speak-Spanish book, some pet medications (which, contrary to what you might expect, did not later show up in his bloodstream), and a slip of pink paper with a phone number written on it. He was not carrying identification. He had some bumps and cuts on his scalp, a throbbing headache, and could think of nothing else to do than turn himself over to the first policeman he saw. He was terrified. Once taken to a local hospital, the doctors ran tests but found nothing wrong with his brain. The nurses commented that he looked different from other people who came into the hospital with no memory—people who were usually dirty, homeless, wild-eyed. But this man was handsome, clean-cut, earnest. When asked to sign some hospital paperwork, he was ecstatic to find that his left hand instinctually began to sign his name with the letter *D*, but then stopped. He could not remember the rest of his own name.

He could not remember, either, that before he lost his memory he had been a successful stockbroker who had made millions of dollars in the stock market while living in Paris, before moving into a luxury New York apartment facing the Empire State Building's sun-glimmering façade. He could not remember that he had quit his job to pursue a new life and career in photography. He could not remember that he had used some of that fortune to travel the world, climbing snowy mountain peaks, surfing waves in exotic locations, dating models in Biarritz. He did not remember that, before he had awoken to his own new childlike, warm-hearted, and mild-mannered disposition, he had been something of a jerk, someone others described as arrogant and cynical. He would later rediscover all of this about himself by following leads from the phone number on the pink slip of paper in his backpack, belonging to a girl he had dated briefly but who had dumped him because she found him too shallow.

The man he had awoken to would never come to identify with the man he once was. That before-man was shrouded in mystery. Incidentally, this man had another inexplicable gap in his life history, during which he had made his enormous fortune. During this time, he had gone missing, unaccounted for. Everyone interviewed about this time in his life, or about how he made so much money, either did not know anything about it or would not comment. Had that man left on a clandestine trip? Had that man committed a crime? Was he *trying* to forget something?

I wanted to know how someone with no evidence of brain trauma could simply lose their entire memory and forget their identity. After seeing the documentary about the Coney Island man, I did some research—for my lecture at first, and then out of pure curiosity—to discover if others had experienced similar *fugue states,* as they were called, and unexplained bouts of memory loss. It appears that, while extremely rare, other people with perfectly healthy brains have suffered similar total retrograde memory loss, meaning they can't remember anything past a certain date. In one case, a 44-year-old Scottish butcher from Aberdeen with no evidence of brain abnormalities experienced an inexplicable attack of amnesia and found himself twelve miles from home after walking for hours. The last thing that he remembered was leaving his house. Then his cell phone rang. He couldn't remember how to answer it. He wandered into a restaurant and was given a ride by a passerby to a bus station where he caught a bus home. His wife came to pick him up at the station, and the look of horror on her face as he stepped off the bus startled him. He thought, "I'll never forget that look."

And for all we know, he didn't forget that look. But he did later forget what his wife looked like in general. He forgot who she was, that he had a wife at all, not to mention two daughters, who he also forgot. Even now, the report says, his memory comes and goes, and it still surprises him every time he sees the look of devastation on the face of someone he doesn't recognize, and that person turns out to be a family member or long-time friend. The damage his loved ones experience from not being remembered haunts him. After one of his worst bouts of amnesia, the butcher from Aberdeen was coming out of the shower as his wife was talking on the phone. She found him in his pajamas, slumped in a corner of the bathroom. He recalls, "I didn't know why I was there like that and I didn't know she was my wife. I didn't know why I was in her house and I wanted to leave." She was crying and he felt bad for her, this stranger before him. But he couldn't help who or what he remembered, he said.

Couldn't *help* it, he said, as though memory were a thing to be assisted or supported, intervened upon. I continued digging to find that in the past two decades, more and more new cases of unexplained amnesia have been documented than ever before. In 1999, a man in his mid-twenties appeared in a Toronto hospital with a broken nose, barely able to walk, and with no memory of who he was or where he had come from. His wallet and identification were missing and all the labels on his clothes had been removed. When they ran tests, the doctors could find no evidence of traumatic brain injury, and could not explain why he had no memory. When it was discovered that he spoke fluent French, Italian, and could read Latin, the media devoured his story and christened him "Mr. Nobody." Later, allegations arose that before he lost his memory he had been a pornographic model in Britain.

Then in 2005, a 20-year-old German man turned up on Kent Beach in England wearing a sodden suit and tie, having no recollection of who or where he was. He was not carrying identification and all of the labels on his clothes had been removed (same as the previous case). When he would not speak during his stay in the hospital, nurses gave him a paper and pen and he drew a piano. When they brought him a piano, he skillfully played Tchaikovsky and songs from the Beatles for hours before they finally took the piano away. He still refused to speak and spent four months in a psychiatric facility, during which time his interpreters and caregivers were contacted by hundreds of newspapers, television networks, interested fans, and orchestras pining to discover his identity and to hear more talent from the memory-less "Piano Man."

In another case—also in England—Sussex policemen found a man lying unconscious and hypothermic between two piers on Brighton beach in early February 2010. The 26-year-old man wore a soaking-wet suit (same as the previous case). He was not carrying identification. He was tall and slim with straight dark hair, and spoke with a perfect English accent (or, as the British newspapers said, with no accent at all). When asked his name, he gave two possible names but said he could not be sure which was his. The police officers doubted the authenticity of the names but "gently" took him into custody. He was in a fragile state, they said. The policemen hoped someone would identify him. Days later they released a report that his fiancée had recognized his picture in the papers and took him home. It was not mentioned whether or not he recognized her back, agreed to go with her, or whether "home" was still, or ever, home for him.

I plowed through these case descriptions as though trying to get to the bottom of a crime. My fascination grew with every story. This was long before we had any news of Grandpa Tom's amnesia. Even after my dad came back from the hospital, I did not immediately draw any connections between these stories and his. I had no immediate reason to compare, as Grandpa Tom's issue was apparently a neurological one. Alcohol had taken a physical toll on his brain. What other explanation was there?

When I had first delved into these other cases, my interest came from a more basic, anthropological curiosity: I wanted to know if it was a coincidence that all of these cases had been either from Europe or the United States. I tried to find cases of total retrograde amnesia in non-Western countries, but found only a sparse few and all were explained by obvious brain trauma, lesions, or congenital abnormalities. Could it be that the kind of acausal amnesia found in the other cases is *culturally*-based? That maybe total retrograde amnesia is the extreme exemplification of a more common Western impulse to forget as a way of moving on? Most non-western cultures don't even have a name or classification for *amnesiac* the way we do, a term that becomes a defining feature of a person's identity when they can't remember their own past. But in our culture, amnesia is a culturally recognized designation comprised of an expected set of features and behaviors that sets the amnesiac apart from others. You aren't just amnesic, you *become* an amnesiac. The cultural script is already there, and if it happens to you, the role somehow slips over you like a silken tunic, draping in all the right places. There are no decisions to be made, and nothing to strategize or consider. Your former self is simply gone. Now, by definition, you are expected to either rediscover who you once were or simply begin again with both the future and the past a yawning blank.

People with amnesia find it hard to imagine the future. This is because the way we imagine and predict the future is closely linked to our memories of earlier experiences. The areas of our brains that are stimulated during fMRI experiments as we envision the future are the same ones that light up when we try to remember the past. These areas of the brain do not just overlap partially, but *completely*, so that it is literally impossible to envision the future without recalling something of the past.

Researchers think that this is an adaptive mechanism that helps us to prepare for future challenges by recognizing patterns across situations we have encountered in the past. The ability to accurately predict how future scenarios might unfold may keep us from walking into oncoming traffic or being eaten by a bear. We know—or can predict with some degree of accuracy—what will happen if we tell an inappropriate joke at a cocktail party or pick a fight with a tall stocky guy at the bar. Maybe we'll lose friends, or get our nose broken. We know because we've seen this happen before—either to us or to someone else, or to someone on TV. Being able to predict uncomfortable or dangerous scenarios allows us to avoid or change them—it helps us, in small but cumulative ways, to survive.

Given this logic, if you can't remember the past, the future is completely uncertain. There are certain benefits to this. Let's consider that the only thing that connects Grandpa Tom to those mysteriously acausal amnesiacs is, well, a *cause*. In Tom's case, the doctors blame alcohol, neurochemicals. This alone is what distinguishes him from the cases of unexplained amnesia. Those other cases could not pinpoint a physical anomaly to explain their memory loss. No lesions, no bumps on the head or skull, no trace of memory-erasing drugs in the bloodstream, *nada*. The only thing that hinges Tom's case to these others is the factor of motive. That I could so easily identify in Grandpa Tom a good reason to forget—this became the pivot-point that led me to consider Grandpa Tom's circumstance in light of the other cases. This, and one other very important thing that my father told me about his visit to Grandpa Tom's facility.

As they walk around the grassy path, Grandpa Tom begins to smile—not the way that he did when my dad first came in, but in a different way, more subtle. It becomes obvious as they're walking that Grandpa Tom's tired brain is grinding and clicking, like an old tractor digesting the earth below. Little by little, Grandpa Tom begins to remember my dad. As my dad is talking, something sets off a firework in Tom's brain. He stops along the pathway and says, "Wait. *YOU'RE*.... *GARY*." Grandpa Tom looks at my dad under his feral eyebrows, and the two of them stand there staring at each other. My dad nods, is fighting back tears because it is like his dad is seeing him for the first time, more fully than he saw him even with his memory intact. This sudden recognition from the hazy depths of Grandpa Tom's recollection seems to carry the full weight of his lack of recognition of my father as his son all these years—not due to amnesia all that time, but something else more cruel—and the weight of it comes swinging round like an anvil for them both. Dad doesn't know what to feel. Is he happy? Tom doesn't know what to feel either, probably, but he is smiling so big, like he's just discovered a goldmine in the caverns of his own brain, like he's setting down the pick-axe after months of climbing aimlessly and staring at the shimmering gold of my father's face and thinking, *bingo*.

That actually happened, Dad says. But what if, now that Grandpa Tom recognizes my dad as his son, he begins to recollect all of the other more painful memories too, the ones that, when pieced together, slowly reveal an image of Grandpa Tom as a mean old drunk? Psychologists have taught us for decades that perceptions of the self as *good* and *right* are among the most motivational needs that humans have. In other words, we are motivated to think of ourselves as other than despicable, even if it means thinking ourselves *into* that someone. The effect of having the full heft of your former self come back to you like a wheelbarrow full of coal dumped at your feet could be psychologically devastating, an impetus for great depression, crisis, the cognitive equivalent of paralysis. Maybe if Tom had to be that person for one more day, he just couldn't go on living. Maybe when the psychological pain is so great, the stakes grow high enough that you don't even have a choice. Consciously or subconsciously, you *have* to make that transformation, or else you'll no longer be able to function, your self-loathing a pair of iron shackles nailing you to the ground. Maybe for people like Grandpa Tom, survival is not in remembering, but in forgetting. By some cryptic, psychodynamic process, you don't even have to think about how to get from person A to person B, it just happens. *That's why the path is there. You don't have to think about where to go.* Another drink, and then another, and you are already putting one foot in front of the other in a miracle of motion.

The way our culture distinguishes illness into Cartesian categories, physical anomalies always trump the psychological or emotional. Identifying a physical cause of Grandpa Tom's memory loss saved everyone—especially his family members and anyone else who really knew him—from having to bother with other potential sources of his memory loss—guilt, shame, fear. These might have implicated a formidable set of reasons for forgetting, thereby calling into question even the most innocent of Grandpa Tom's memory lapses. It might have removed Tom's amnesia from the realms of inevitability—a consequence of "wet brain" or lesions or physical trauma—into a realm of choice, however subconscious. Still, even biomedicine does not understand very well the boundaries between the physical and the psychological. Indeed, most neurologists and biologists now argue that one is inextricably linked to the other, and that our state of mind is intimately tied to our biochemistry, just as our biochemistry is intimately influenced by our mood and responses to external events. Given our current knowledge, it is impossible to delineate where our emotions and cognition leave off and our neurochemistry and biology begin. The proverbial chicken and egg dilemma ensues with as much force as it did a hundred or even five hundred years ago.

When the doctors say, then, that Grandpa Tom's amnesia is due entirely to Wernicke-Korsakoff syndrome, I can't help but ask: *All of it?* And if not all of it, then *How much?* He did, after all, begin to remember my father after just one visit, which indicates that his memories were not simply erased. They remained somehow hidden in the folds of his current experience, perhaps coloring his emotional reactions in ways that even he could not explain or understand.

What had changed was not the existence of the memories themselves, but Grandpa Tom's capability—or desire—to access them.

This kind of subterfuge would seem to take a lot of work and meticulous planning. One might think that the brain of an alcoholic like Grandpa Tom isn't capable of the difficult cognitive leaps and masterful self-deceptions it might take to pull off a real identity switch—one that not only others believe but that you believe, too, utterly convinced that you are no longer that man from before. But I came across a study from the 1990s showing that while chronic heavy drinking can significantly impair the memory, it does not result in the loss of gray matter—the *thinking* part of the brain. This means that Grandpa Tom's strategizing skills remained intact throughout what I call his "blanking" episode, and still do to this day.

And what about the bizarre details of the other cases, that nearly all of them carried no identification, with one man missing even the most trivial of identifiers—the labels ripped from his clothing? Did he rip those labels off himself? Did everyone just coincidentally forget their I.D.s at home the day they blanked out? And why had they all been walking around so long, miles away from home? Can't one have a "fugue state" in their own neighborhood or backyard, circling the barbecue pit or the community pool? The more I consider the details of these cases, the more I see a certain intelligence revealed in the ways these men parted with their previous selves.

This kind of intelligence, however, might not be a conscious one. In the same way that Freud posited a kind of psychodynamic, unconscious intelligence that leads us to adaptively transform negative thoughts of ourselves or our mothers and fathers into more manageable and psychosocially acceptable pathologies (or dream-objects, etc.), so might we possess an unconscious intelligence that allows us to forgive ourselves and move on. Or just to simply move on.

As far as Grandpa Tom goes, the undeniable facts are that the physiological effects of excessive drinking culminated in the gradual degradation of the nutrients his brain needed to inform his sense of self in a space approximating reality. He didn't *decide* to forget, orchestrating some sort of auto-heist of his own memories. It is clear from a biomedical perspective that the alcohol made him forget. But what made the alcohol travel down his throat, settle into his veins, steadily lap away at the shore of his fragile neurons? How many micro-decisions to unscrew, pour, sip, swallow does it take to add up to a larger, more-unconscious decision to forget? And what about his openness to the memories that do begin to resurface?

I wonder to what extent these are carefully vetted at a level that is out of even Grandpa Tom's consciousness, allowed to pass into conscious memory according to a variety of psychosocial contingencies more complex than Tom could ever hope to imagine or understand, but which allow him to effectively survive in the absence of total despair.

Even if deep down I don't believe that he is consciously faking the whole phenomenon of his memory loss in an effort to reconnect with family in his last, dying days, I can't help but acknowledge that becoming another person overnight has certain consequences that could be conceived as beneficial, even if inseparable from their obvious devastations. I wonder if the *thinking* part of Grandpa Tom's brain recognizes this too.

If you look at the other cases, the benefits of memory loss seem to outweigh many of the detriments. Of the "unknown white male" who woke up from his fugue to find that he was a rich man but no longer obliged to assume the less-than-enviable personality of the before-man who had made him rich, people said he had become nicer and more introspective, with an "almost-mystical charisma." A friend said, "It was like dealing with a child." After his memory loss, he rebuilt afresh many of the relationships he had with people in his former life, including his girlfriend. Because his story was so incredible, he became a darling of Manhattan socialites and celebrities, scoring invitations to parties and dinners by the likes of the singer Bjork, the director Spike Jonze, and the actor Vincent D'Onofrio. Everyone wanted him to tell his story, and so the Coney Island amnesiac told it, over and over.

"Are you buying this?" asked someone who had met him at a party, speaking to a mutual acquaintance. He thought that it seemed strange how every conversation became an opportunity for the man to tell his captivating story of amnesia. If someone played an album by the Rolling Stones, the man would say, "Who is this? Is this a new band?" and someone would look at him incredulously and this would launch the story all over again.

In the case of the Piano Man, the man's identity was confirmed with the help of the German foreign ministry and he was released from the psychiatric facility. Shortly after, it was discovered that in previous years leading up to his amnesic episode, the Piano Man had bombarded German television stations and pleaded with celebrities to help launch his career in music, but to no avail. He had come back to Britain on a train after losing his job in Paris. Four months after his mysterious bout of amnesia, the man spontaneously recovered his memory. To his stunned parents, he said: "I have no idea what happened. I've just suddenly woken up and realized who I was."

By the time the Piano Man remembered who he was, he had already garnered the attention and fascination of the public eye. He admitted that when the police found him on the beach, he had been planning to commit suicide. It is not known whether he remembers why, or what happened to him out there as he drifted through the cold water. Maybe it was something like what happened to Grandpa Tom right before he landed himself in the hospital.

"Sometimes he gets violent," the nurse told Dad the day he visited. The words swam in Dad's ears as the nurse walked him across the sterile-looking lobby, past the reception desk, the tangled plants nesting in their pots, down the echoing, clip-cloppy hallway. *Violent*. Dad already knew this about Tom. The nurses said that he often refused help, refused food, demanded to know when he would be set free.

I am not surprised to hear that Grandpa Tom gets violent—even now, even here, even the new Grandpa Tom who, teary-eyed, embraced my dad as his son for the first time, while the birds chirped in the trees and the sun shone overhead. Maybe it is because I can remember the past that it seems so easy to predict the future. I predict that Tom will live for another five or seven years, remembering just enough, the way children selectively remember the best parts of the story, letting duller details fall away. I predict that Dad will try to get to know the new Tom, and that Tom will both look for and drop hints in conversation that he and my father have some deeper connection, more substantial than the same blood type. I predict Tom will gradually begin to remember who he once was, who my father is, and that Tom's resentment will slowly creep back, his self-loathing and whatever drove him to blank in the first place. Because I believe that Tom is still there, floating beneath the surface of his memory loss, like a sunken canoe growing buoyant with algae.

Until then, what a strange relief for my father to walk into Tom's room and see his memory dissipated into a kind of dust you see floating around in rays of sunlight—some bits of substance there, but nothing sticking together. The two men come to know a new, indefinable levity. ❦

Advice for writers?

I'll answer with a challenge I faced with this essay about my dad, how he suffered for my grandpa's bad decisions and neglect. Behind this family story, I explore (my dad might say "intellectualize") how much agency we have in "forgetting." Deeper still, the essay is also about how much agency I—as a writer—have to tell the story how I want to. In journalism, they call it "integrity." But in nonfiction, is there a name for how we are obliged to storytell? Elsewhere, I've called it "sincerity," a need to soften our will to "forge" a truth about what something means for us. But must we also to be true to what it means for others? When my dad suggested I change my essay's last line to better reflect the solemnity of never finding the dad he'd searched so long for, I thought long and hard. I decided instead to leave the reader with the impression (more in line with my "thesis," you could say) that grandpa's "blanking" afforded both men some levity after such gravity. Should I have changed it? My advice would be answer to that question in your own writing.

Kristin Kostick

NEW MILLENNIUM
AWARD FOR NONFICTION

Blanking by Kristin Kostick

Kristin Kostick is a poetry and nonfiction writer currently working on a collection of essays called *You Not You* about the advantages of self-deception. She is also a medical anthropologist researching bioethics and health policy at Baylor College of Medicine in Houston.

LEARN MORE AT KRISTINKOSTICK.COM.

POETRY SUITE
2019

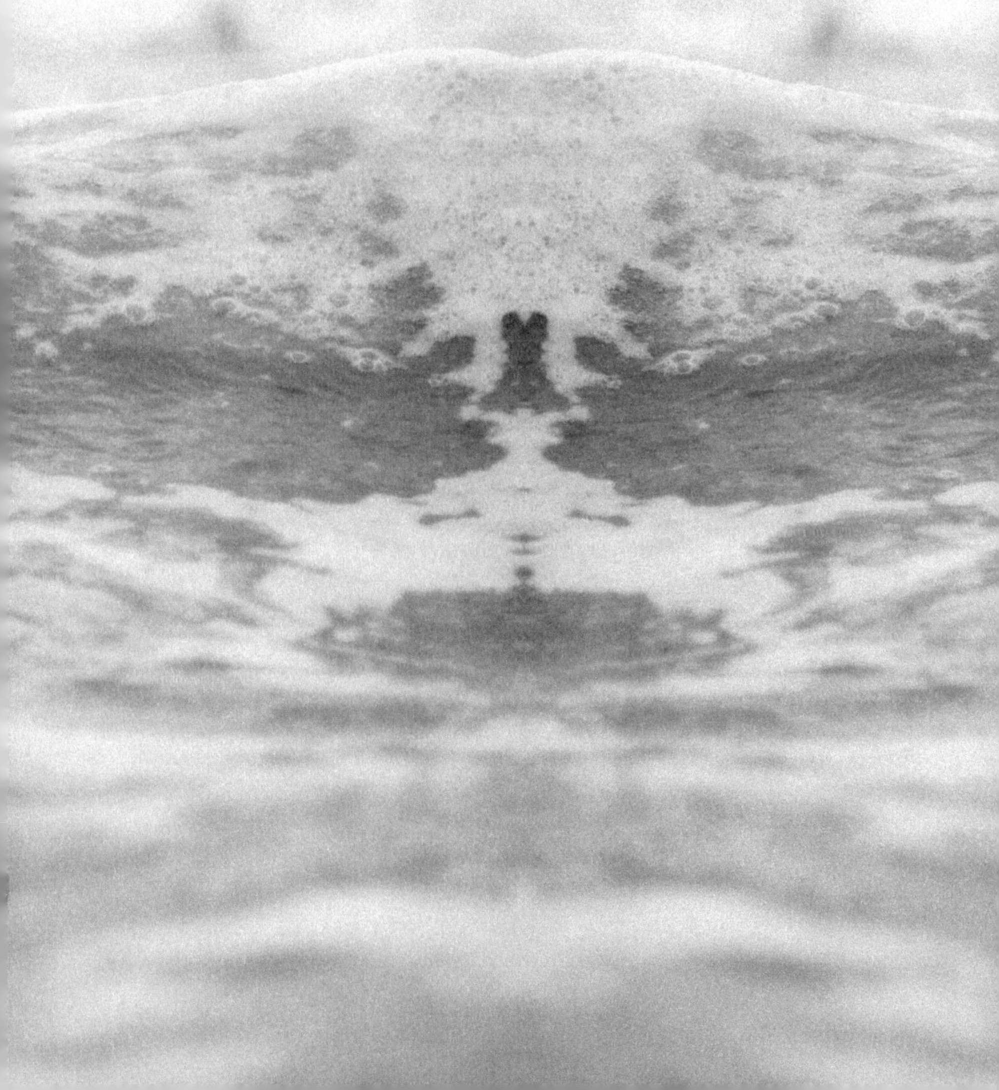

Kemmer Anderson

ANCIENT ADDICTIONS: THE COLERIDGE CONNECTION

based on drawings by Alan Farrant

The cross and bow war within my brain
string every nerve, bend bones, pull muscles,
stretch skin across the target
where the needle searches for the vein.

The pen's prick sticks through epidermis layers
where language covers up pain
with myth and lyric oozing through the pores
until the eye draws the word out through a syringe.

Who can dwell below the cognate spirit
that shapes the mind into a sea of need?
Desire laps against the appetite
with an anorexic revenge for one last supper

while this sin stares ever before me
with an addict's eye shut to light.
Tied to a mast without beeswax in my ears
I hear the fish and gull talk about you and me

until we grow gills, fins, and scales then dive
beneath the text where fear coagulates into scabs
of archetype seen at the bottom of the bottle
where the sea writes your epitaph in squid's ink.

"Not a drop to drink," you say, Coleridge.
Yet to withdraw from this bottled pride
will be the death of me when my breath
no longer needs this last swallow.

I could fix another drink—the last one
or let the crucifix draw desire out. I thirst.
The forms rise between the waves in a Socratic dance.
On the horizon lines divide these lies into visible

and invisible objects of bread and wine.
Where is this port for living water? How do I draw water
From a shapeless well of salt water?
The keeper of the maps is coming.

The navigator turns his compass. A dizzy fire infects the blood.
Images rise and fall in protean shifts of consciousness.
Metaphor swallows morphine.
The dead still speak in forgotten syllables.

Phonemes break into prayers so common
that even the fish and fowl know the words.
The albatross in me waits to be
released during this migration toward sound.

Jacqueline Berger

MORAL INJURY

Grainy feed on the flat screen—
cloudy skies ten thousand miles away,
so it's hard to tell who is enemy
and who a child with a stick
or a woman carrying laundry.
Somewhere in a suburb of a suburb,
soldiers who once were boys,
disembodied gamers long past bedtime,
but women as well in these rooms.
No need to wear fatigues,
it's a desk job after all, but they do.
Other times they follow the known enemy
for days, watch him eating dinner
with his family, playing catch before dark.
Take anyone off the battlefield
and he is human. Which doesn't mean,
of course, he doesn't deserve to die.
The button pushed, the target killed.
Which doesn't mean it isn't fun.
Wander down the hall for a soda.
Each swig roughed up by grit, sand,
shards, or the fine powder of bones.
Soon it is time for lunch.

All at once, the butterflies have hatched.
In the buckeye, closed fans
snapping open as they alight.
June, and the clothesline drags
under the weight of winter's jackets.
Not the threat of bodily injury
but its absence—soldiers calling air
to deliver a strike—the safety
of the killing room that crawls

under their skin, two fingers
tenting flesh for the injury
to enter and seek asylum.
An upward shower when
the butterflies lift off and the sky
explodes with blinking scraps of gold.

FJ Bergmann

THIS TIME

... and she was one of the damosels of the lake, that hight Nimue. But Merlin would let her have no rest, but always he would be with her. And ever she made Merlin good cheer till she had learned of him all manner thing that she desired; and he was assotted upon her ...

—Sir Thomas Malory, *Le Morte Darthur*

of year you can see to the bottom of the lake.
No woman's arm. No gleaming sword. I return
once every century to maintain the accords of trust,
ever-delaying the reckoning, the summoning.

Two doors lie before me: one into light and one
into shadow; I choose neither. I am he who waits.
When I am hungry, I devour diesel-stained air
like an accordion, scrape condensation from glass

windowpanes, windshields, mirrors. I still possess
a hedge-magician's array of tricks: anyone can
learn to swallow a sword, to eat fire, to inhale
a lit fuse back into oneself until its glow is no more

than an invisible shimmer. But no more disciples.
In the old days, the powerful took what they wished:
that was the natural order. And they were expected
to reward their lovely assistants as they deemed fit

... foolishly forgetting that Fate is also a woman.
Ah, Nimue, what reward did either of us deserve?
You, for your betrayal; I, for what in this new age
would be termed your exploitation. And both of us

under the yoke of loyalty to a transformed kingdom.
Queendom, I hear you whisper. Arthur still sleeps.

Title and first line from the last sentence of "Guard? Guard!" by Ed Skook, Poetry, *October 2017*

Sarah Blanchard

OPTATIVE DREAMING

Oh that I may become a corpse, my child, instead of you!
—Euripedes, Hippolytus

Who invented the wish,
the desire for a thing that cannot or will not happen?

And who created regret,
those shameful second guesses born of haste and rash decisions?

We live in parallels,
imaging the conditional past or present or future.
Here's a wishing well in an echo chamber,
offering shoulda woulda coulda for a penny or nothing.

The optative mood is futile desire, nostalgic regret, powerless prayer
dismissed by the gods.

Floating forward from the past,
insincere platitudes can proliferate safely.
Letter to an angry lover: I wish I had been a kinder, gentler person.

Camped in the present,
useless thoughts safely marry things that cannot be true.
Postcard from Hawai'i: Wish you were here

Leaning into the future,
desperation finds an impossible voice.
News of Somalia: If only it would rain, they might survive.

If wishes were horses, then beggars might ride.
If only, what could've been, so maybe now—
If so, all would be different.

I might as well suppress a heartfelt sigh
and say, I wish I'd been born in the age of Euripides.

The cat is both alive and dead until someone opens the box.
If I knew her name, I would tell you.

Constance Campana

INCIDENT, 2015: THE NEWSCASTER ASKS THE VICTIMS TO CONSIDER OUTSIDE CIRCUMSTANCES

He asked them how they felt about the policeman drawing a gun on them now that they knew the policeman had come from two attempted suicide calls, one after the other, to their swimming pool party where teenagers in bathing suits had been invited—black and white teenagers—though only the black ones were thrown down and only one, a girl, 15, wouldn't stay down—her long black hair, orange bikini—her flawless dark skin—seen over and over on the news as the policeman held her wrist to her back until she finally stayed, her face turned in the grass, and everyone heard her calling, her mouth open, and saw three boys rush to her—a miracle, really—and then the cop, coming from two suicides pulled out his gun and the boys fled— —how do you feel, the victims were asked, now that you know the whole story?

He shouldn't have answered the call—he shouldn't have been in charge and it was then that we heard the voices of children remembering the sudden shift to violence and we saw them again in their bathing suits and like them we thought he should not have come at all.

Like the newsman, I have tried to see things wholly wanting to believe it possible. But you never forget the change in light, you never forget the gun, do you.

Shuyu Cao

奴: SLAVE

i pray for my barren emperor, shriveled in temptations. blood from
my pious knees permeated cracked yellow dirt, fertilized terra cotta. in
image of myself, i sculpted an army of royal blood, birthing dynasties
from my insolence. sons accompany me down a tomb so bewitching, my
lords, you dare not open. you uncover my earth like artifact.

i decorate my daughter zhaojun for her second wedding. phoenix pin,
needle, umbilical cord, thread, weaving message into her scalp: sparrows
will not fly south this year. i teach her to give pleasure but do not teach
her to give birth, the things that make us women. dont fret, your flesh
will rot when he unravels the life your head. i birthed a rock, burned to
gold, praise me, i turned concubine to heroine.

i water mongolian plains with kumis leaked from my swollen nipples,
my son Temujin trampled my vegetable patch during a drunken tribal
brawl. i forgave him. when he flashed silver against his brothers neck, i
pulled out my forsaken breasts. spill one drop of my milk flowing in his
veins and this good earth will revolt against you. i saved sixteen million.

i dripped my whores virgin menses along our journey to the west. at the
doors of shaolin, our punctuated cries of rape evaporated in vairocanas
empty palms. from our bloated uteruses, i carved my buddha face
into the mountains. my whores labored in music of ecstasy. the monk
trembled under his robe.

i weaved a silk whip laced in opium to pleasure meiji king. collecting
blood droplets budding on his lips, i concocted plum blossom wine
stronger than poison. sun drank. sun wept.

i am slave artist count the strokes in my body woman, half the name

Jack Cooper

BY WAY OF CRYING

It had been a bruising day and I went to bed
wondering if I had said thank you enough

since saying thank you is like looking up at the stars
the more you see the more there is

and the more thankful you feel about being part of it all
So I said thanks to Theodore Roethke for his line that I'd recently read

(and somehow missed years ago)
"I long for the imperishable quiet at the heart of form"

That's a thought that lives on
from a poet who died too young some would say

I thanked the woman on the Red Line home from work
who asked me for a quarter

How often I turn from such requests without listening
(on the runaway train of assumption)

This time I waited for the whole story
as she smiled by way of crying from her mouth full of holes

She only wanted to buy an apple because
she was having the rest of her teeth extracted the very next day

and afraid she might never again be able to bite the forbidden fruit
I understood that the seventy-five cents I found in my backpack

would be enough since she must have said thank you ten times
I also wanted to tell my friend B. how grateful I was

that he'd called for my help and listened to my advice
(When was the last time that happened?)

I had urged him to write a book on his discordant odyssey in a life of music
and I knew the first chapter had to be the day he discovered

his dad's shimmering trombone in a velvet-lined case in the garage
and dropped his piano lessons like a bad note to become a horn player

on a path of delayed mastery as an orchestral conductor
(Was there still time?)

To get him started I mailed him my notes from our conversation
A friend can help you start something impossible because

a friend can go to the heart of your form
And then there was L. who sent me an email

saying he'd read somewhere that I'd died
and was wondering if I was okay or not

I wrote him back saying it was all true
and he wouldn't believe the imperishable quiet on the other side

But I forgot to thank him for thinking of me
Saying thanks makes you forget we're all supposed to die someday

James Cooper

CLINICAL NOTE TEMPLATE FOR MEN IN THERAPY

Now in our _____ year, we sail in (circle one) turbulent/calm/turquoise seas. We used to talk of labor and construction, but we've left the sandstone gorges and ruined cities. We've left the palaces, overgrown by vines. We're aware of childhood treasures nibbling on present thoughts. I'm curious about the contradiction between his (circle one) tenuous/tenacious leaning way, and his actual choice of words. Our guts are involved, our customary expressions buffeted by currents. We navigate potential space, but neither of us can see our event horizon. Shame is guarded by __________. He wonders if he can sustain love, and what he took as evidence of love from his mother. He knows, in a formless way, why his father __________.

He doubts anyone cares about his smaller wounds. He wants to rest by a fallen tree near a quiet creek. I sense a surge of his enigmatic __________. It hits me as a glaring theme in my own life. We feel an uneasy recognition, but I must remember; his path is not mine. I'm careful not to comment when he needs to freely roam. Gender follows us from past generations. We fight the categories. He's been looking intently at the __________, tucked away in my bookshelf. By now, it's acquired a private meaning.

I'm looking for a missing chapter. He reports an urgent need to see __________. He's reluctant to tell me, says he's much better anyway. A squall is on the horizon. I try to protect the space we've worked to create. He speaks of __________for the first time. We're deep in this mysterious business. We'll meet again on Thursday night, but if the moon is full and orange, we'll speak of little else.

Alice Ashe

SOME THINGS THAT COME IN TWOS

front teeth, your
crooked eyes &

mouths, attached
I love you (too)

pink lines
on a stick

in tarot: cups
& swords

heartbeats, soft
& strong

shoes, here
& gone

not parents

fingers
forming
peace

Lisa Dordal

WELCOME

Flipping the remote, I keep landing
on the hotel's Welcome Channel.

Hello, a woman says. White woman,
pretty smile. *May I have a minute of your time?*

Be as alert as you are at home, she says.
Pretty woman, concerned for my safety.

She keeps walking towards me—there,
behind everything else. Like fear behind the eyes.

I keep flipping, taking in the news of the week.
People are protesting in the streets:

This Pussy Fights Back. No Ban, No Wall.
Never invite strangers into your room.

Pretty smile, pretty woman. As pretty
as my mother was when she was alive.

Pretty as she was in my dream. Be alert,
the woman says. *As alert as you are at home.*

I never knew, on Tuesdays, what she'd look like—
my mother, who drove to the Del Mar College

of Hair Design to get dolled up cheap
by a stranger. Sometimes, large, loopy curls.

Other times, tight and small—tucked in
like something sleeping. *Use the viewport,*

the woman says, *if someone knocks on your door.*
Hepburn-chestnut one week to a sassy blonde

the next. In the dream, she is reading
from my book. She looks happy.

Keep the doors and windows locked,
the woman says. In five pages,

my mother will be dead. First, the bottles
hidden in bookcases throughout

the house. Then, the heart wing. *Locked,*
the woman says, *at all times.* My mother

glances up. She is reading in the voice she used
for *Sounder* and *The Chronicles of Narnia.*

She reads as if the woman she is
will not die; as if the woman who dies

will not be her. As if she is not even *there.*
Like when she learned about my attempts—

aspirin, then the knife, my hand like Abraham's
over Isaac. *Nice story,* my mother said.

We had learned to slip out of ourselves.
To squeeze our consciousness through a hole

the size of a dime. We were small inside
our bodies. My body is sin, she told me once.

Be alert, the woman says. *As alert*
as you are at home. Nice story, she said.

First appeared in Ninth Letter, *Summer 2017*

C.W. Emerson

STOPOVER ON A ROAD TRIP TO L.A., 1981

Didn't I stand there once,
nineteen, loose-limbed,

dripping water onto the catwalk
above the motel pool?

And weren't we luminous then?—
our bodies glistening,

younger than the slice of moon
hung in a Vegas sky.

And wasn't there a door, a threshold,
one simple, white-walled room?

Didn't we taste the peyote's fire,
christen ourselves with totemic names?—

Wouldn't I become *grey wolf,*
bitter oleander, monkshead, moss?

And you would have been
bobcat, lily of the valley, my love,

salt cedar, eucalyptus—
if only you'd lived a little longer.

Sam Griswold

THE HOUSE I WISH I GREW UP IN

There's a house I wish I grew up in
sometimes, on the bank of a river, or a stream,
where at dusk the light from the windows
catches hold and casts shadows through the
branches of the trees and the rusty gate
and things start to disappear.

A gravel road winds to it through the woods,
disperses like a ship's wake, echoing
before headlights come into view,
an old projector churning to life behind a curtain,
something out of a novel I've stumbled into,
familiar because it's not mine.

There's mystery here, I can sense it,
beneath the ice I glide upon careful,
afraid of staying still, or amidst the
patches of darkness and the moss-covered graves
that I run from and the smoke from the chimney
on the far bank that I've never seen.

I often think of it at dusk—
the thought always makes me homesick.

C.W. Emerson

AFTER VISITING THE LOURDES OF LEBANON

St. Charbel, born Youssef Makhlouf in 1828, lived as a hermit in the Maronite Order in northern Lebanon. The oil that leaks from his burial site is said to possess miraculous healing powers.

I went, as you asked,
            to Saint Charbel's tomb—
flew first to Beirut,
then traveled by bus
to the city of Byblos
and back again,
returning to you
with a vial in my hands.
I poured the precious oil
over your limbs, prayed
it would seep into brittle bone
and slow the cells growing there

                        by infinite degree,

to less than the velocity

                                    of the faintest breath.

*

I toggle back and forth
between faith and doubt,
            no right or wrong
to this kind of thing.
You tell me to pray,
            and reluctantly, I do.

My holy grammar lifts
to where lace of cloud
meets mountain face,

then higher still:

by the grace of the saints,

return him to me.

*

There's no need to outlive me
or any of the others.
Just make your way down
to the ground floor
and out to your old Renault.
I've primed the engine for you,
turned it over, warmed the seat.
Roll down the window
and listen to its music
as it tick-tick-ticks
down street after street

into next year,

and the next,

and the next.

Robert Evory

SYMPATHY VIBRATION

There was a father who had a son, wanted to tell him all the reasons for the things he's done.

—Paul Simon

Maybe I will see my father again
in the faces of my children.
Maybe I won't be able to recognize my wife.
But I will be able to sing this song.

I am singing it to myself now,
at home, no children yet
cooking dinner for my wife.

Every time I sing the word *Father*:
which is high for my register,
which sounds a missing ghost of breath
in my diaphragm
drawn out longer than other words
I match the harmonic frequency of the doorbell.

So the bell would vibrate and ring.
Everything makes a sound, everything vibrates.

A pitch fork plays an *A*
when you hit it,
but also if you sing an *A*
to the pitch fork
it will sing an *A* back—
like children repeating my dirty words and habits.

My father taught me to play the song on guitar
and I make it a point to teach
my music students who don't know

who Paul Simon is.
Try explaining hippies
to a catholic school girl gymnast, age twelve.
Because she asks, and says her dad says
they did drugs and broke the law—
try explaining a cultural revolution in 30 minutes
while also strumming a Bolero Rhythm.

When I first sang and heard my doorbell,
it was a revelation.
I thought I found my voice.
I thought my throat finally
unsubmerged itself.

I soon realized the sympathy vibration was coming
from another place in the house, from the doorbell,
that it wasn't leaving me like a sun flair
whose radiation turns into light in the atmosphere of earth—though it might be close.

The electronic part of myself:
that makes me sing
also makes the doorbell ring,

that human impulse of nerve and synaptic charge
that forms every move, thought, decision, and sound

made the bell,
made for asking to enter

through the mouth of my home,
sing for a father and his son.

Ed Frankel

GUELAGUETZA

At the stoplight of the Overland entrance
to the Santa Monica Freeway going West,
a woman is standing on the four-foot wide median
that separates traffic, selling bags of oranges
and peanuts from a shopping cart,
single stemmed crimson roses.
She walks up and down, peering
over the flowers into the drivers' windows.
I try to figure how much she makes
on each two dollar bag of oranges,
each two dollar long stemmed rose.

I buy a rose, a bag of oranges and some peanuts,
tell her keep the change from the twenty and wish her well .
At home I put the rose in a glass of water.
and think about my own atravesados,
my own crossers of borders—Luftmenschen—
people who could live on air as they traveled,
with their hearts trussed with twine and old rope,
clutchers of lean bones,
their valises stuffed with stale bread, hard, long-shots,
posed sepia memories in stiff borrowed clothes,
clutchers of thin straws and last hopes,
who didn't wear necklaces of marigolds and sugar skulls
but maybe one of rozhinkes mit mandlin,
raisins and almonds,
who didn't drink champurado made from corn and chocolate
but glasses of tea with a lumps of sugar between their teeth.

In Russia, they were pickers and sellers,
who bought pins, needles paper and string
for a ruple and sold them for a ruple and a half,
who stood on their toes to reach God's ear
beyond the pale of settlement.

Rockers in the lap of steerage.
Venders and hawkers
wheeling pushcarts on the cobblestones
instead of shopping carts by the freeway.
They were luchenkups — noodle headed dreamers.

I want to see you again Juana,
face to face, no glass between us.
I want this poem to be my ofrenda to you,
Guelaguetza — and an offering for my people of the air.
That these words like your corn stalks and sugar cane
arch across the years to provide an alter in time
a space to lay out my luftmenschen's pictures,
their favorite things, and their mementos.

My father's stiff, sweat stained handball gloves,
A picture of him, at Hickum Field, Pearl Harbor,
his campaign hat cocked and jaunty,
behind his fifty caliber machine gun in nineteen forty;
My Aunt Molly's button from the Ladies Garment Workers' Union,
her picture taken in 1911 during the strikes
as she marches arm in arm with the other women;
My Zade Izzy's copy of *Huckleberry Finn* and his English dictionary;
a picture of my uncle Joe, playing in the Harry James band,
the mouthpiece from his silver Benge, standing at attention.
No moles and sweet tamales,
but maybe varnishkes with kasha and potato latkas.
No mescal but maybe some shnapps or some Cherry Kijafa.
After they've eaten they will look for me
to leave their good will and their blessings.

Juana, you won't remember the gavacho
who watched you by the freeway and wished you well.
who saw his grandparents in your place
selling flowers by the freeway
instead of vegetables and fish on Hester Street,

who saw his Luftmenschen sewing in a maquiladora
instead of the sweatshops in New York in 1911,
who had the audacity to imagine you dancing
with a necklace of sugar skulls and marigolds,
and then another of raisins and almonds.
Foregive him his audacity,
hijo de la gente del aire.
He comes by it honestly, and he means no harm.
He too is a luftmensch,
another noodle-headed dreamer.

Guelaguetza: a Zapotec offering, a gift to share or reciprocate

Ofrenda: offering

Gavacho: Caucasian- American

Varnishkes mit kasha and potato latkas: bow-tie noodles, bulgar wheat and potato pancakes

Maquiladora: sweat shop

Hijo de La Gente del Aire: a son of the people of the air

Trish Lindsey Jaggers

MIGRANT

Doesn't the body know the transplanted heart aches
for simple symbiosis, its raw self lifted out
of another's sinking boat? Its new craft
now christened a pirate's ship—pillaging vessels and cells—
a chest of mercy once thrown overboard, cracked open. This heart wants
nothing more than to live, too, take little from the rivers
cutting through it, give everything to the oceans waiting at the edge,
embrace the commensal gathering of breaths. Fed and awed.
Not rejection. Hearts cannot beat rejection.

Michele Harris

INSTINCT

The blast furnace's coke fires heaving with light:
Roger dumps in coal, limestone flux, iron ore, each shovelful
coughed back in sparks, orange light thrown up

for miles, and heat, such heat that Roger's sweat
turns to steam, burns off him
in blisters, softens the blue shirt he'll rip off

in the shower, where dozens of bare gray bodies
huddle like fish, the sulfur water sluicing off
salt, stinging cold. Today he'll go home

to casserole and cold cuts. Last Thursday, his wife
packed him a tuna sandwich with pickles and mustard,
her small knuckled hands dicing

through the wheezy downbeats of *Don't Explain*
when the cutting board slipped and the knife left
a jagged red seam on her thumb. She brought it

to her mouth, the penny taste of it, the comfort of blood
staying in her body. Roger remembers
that day by smell, on his lunch break

chewing his soft sandwich, taking in the fishy taste
watching cast houses where slag
oozed down, lava black, even the air

hissing with heat
when Ed Phillips tripped
over a half-filled palette

and fell onto a ream of cooling steel, glowing half-red—
how there was screaming but not
from Ed, who didn't have time when flames

tore through him, first his chest then legs then head,
the black smoke and white steam
hissing out of him. No one helped

because they couldn't.
It took three hours for the steel
to cool enough to wheel him out. The foreman tried to pull

the tar of his body free with a crowbar.
The men went home early. Roger told his wife
nothing, and by instinct Jenny knew

to make halushki and kissel, knew
to bring him to her mouth.

Elizabeth Jackson

CONSTELLATIONS

In a basement box, I rediscover my map
of the night sky   that cardboard wheel
from twenty years ago, his gift

of constellations   rotated into view.
Midnight walks, fields of knee-high grass;
our bodies glowed argent, attraction
like gravity   grounding.   Am I now the marrying kind?

My computer   telescopes distance   his face close
enough to touch   that wide-bowed smile still
impossibly bright— ghost light.

And there's his wife, Marguerite,   snug
in the crook of one arm;   two boys
encircle them   laughing.
My cat saunters in front,   commands

my hand,   completing it, fingers and palm
following curves—head, neck, back—
waves of creamsickle silk.

Even my tabby can't stay the pull,
this house-dark like a black hole.   What escape?
Another world— movie, bar,
a too-young friend,   the distraction

of his muscled chest, the heat
of bourbon, neat.   We origami napkins,
concoct horoscopes, and beside my car

under faint stars, he invites me
to his apartment, eyes unblinking, still
with hope, I could lose
traveling the past.

The moon deceives. It's not a porthole,
not even a slice of celestial life Isn't it just a view
of borrowed light?

AKaiser

AT THE SPEED OF LIGHT, SQUARED

Clairsentience: an extremely heightened form of empathy that transcends boundaries of both space and time. It cannot be compelled to happen in the laboratory or on command.

I thought of this while we two waited for Grace, our
    acupuncturist, your foot so badly
black and blued from kicking a stone stair with all

your might, not realizing the friend had already pulled
    the ball away. Her office all soft
lights and muted *erhu* notes. Curtain ripple, she's here.

We go through the healing we had tried to accelerate
    since our last visit. Changes
in pain, swelling become inert – despite the massages

and the Chinese ointment we mixed with good faith,
    water then wine. I thought how
is it that I did not feel you hitting your foot hitting

immoveable stone that afternoon of extra recess me
    working a mere .5 miles away?
How is it that I did not feel that, if, when she grabbed

your foot and bent it in the direction you had explained
    still hurt, I felt, again,
the ring of fire I had felt ten years previous when you

crowned your head through me to this outside world?

Sandy Longley

SOLACE AT THE P.O.

So, it's my turn and I place an envelope
on the counter. The clerk asks:

"Does this package contain any hazardous liquid?"
Only a thousand tears, I reply.

"Is there anything flammable or breakable?"
Just my heart, I say.

"Would you like this sent express mail
for an additional $7.50?"
Actually, I'd prefer a slow delivery,
maybe in a canvas saddlebag, on a
dappled mare, rambling through mountains,
through valleys lush and deep, pausing
for long drinks in stony creeks.

"How about insurance?"
We both know there's no insurance,
no deductible, for matters like this;
I know what I have given,
what I have received.

He glances at the customer line lengthening–
impatience spreading like a virus.

I want him to close his window and ask me
to meet him out back. He'll be wearing cowboy
boots and smell like fresh cut locust burl.

He'll drape his tattooed arm (wild boar)
around me, offer a cigarette and say
"A dog walks into a bar..."

Barbara Mossberg

WHEN I DIE YOU DON'T HAVE TO DIVERT THE RIVER FOR ME

Fragments of an epic text found in Me-Turan (modern Tell Haddad) relate that at the end of his life Gilgamesh was buried under the river bed. The people of Uruk diverted the flow of the Euphrates passing Uruk for the purpose of burying the dead king within the river bed.

But it would be nice. The river I am thinking of is the Merced, of course, River of Mercy, flowing as Sierras' melted snow cascading in waterfall over rocks in its bed so shiny and clean, the water so clear, it is as if the vanity of earth, which loves rivers, is redeemed here, in how the bark and leaves of trees and shimmer of blue sky and white clouds manifest in its surface, a river the color of spring leaves, a warm yellow, a gold, a bronze—the rocks tell you everything—John Muir says they sing, they preach—this river I have lain beside and leaped into, or rather, hopped, on the gleaming gold-stuff in the sand, and the wind in the willows, on an afternoon in Yosemite, by the chapel, and my father's ashes in this stream, and my mother's—and to get me underneath this river, so that it flows over me, you would have to enlist the moon to move closer, you could do that, it loves music, you could get someone to play the cello, and a flute, and it would come close, as it does when it thinks no one is watching—that's why we get these moments when the earth seems to stop for a moment, and your ears fill—and the water would leap up like a trout, arc for the fly moon, and in that moment, you would have hampers, not for the water, but for the picnic for the people who have come to watch and say, cheerfully, "I love hard work, I could watch it for hours," and they would be eating Julia Child's train sandwiches, loaves with unsweetened butter and ham that have been sat on for the journey, and are now squashed, with gherkins, and raspberries smelling of soap, and some whiskey, the water would arch over the picnickers in a stream like a rainbow, you would get your team with shovels to quickly dig into the fools' gold river bottom and its rocks, and make a little dent for my bones. Meanwhile the river is now on the other side of the meadow, but as I said, you don't have to divert the river. It will spring back of its own accord, and will rush over my spirit alive again today in the trout's freckles and the rock's speckles and star matter.

Damen O'Brien

THE DARKNESS

Caramel in the sauce,
the ointment closing under an eyelid,
the spinnakerluffing at the centre of an eye,
the stripe measuring a tiger,
the fat in the lion's roar,
the shy creature hiding under a rock
that slips away into the patches of a chessboard
before the rock is lifted,
the homecoming promised in a hug,
the gentle marrow growing in the night.

We fear the unknown so much
we wish to understand it,
we shine torches into the dark and
scoop out the caverns of mystery
so that there is nothing there
but loss drying its new wings.

Leavened as the silver under a tongue,
where will men and women hawk their myths
rising like a bubble in a syrup of dreams?
The Old Dark pours his whispered tales
into the ears of sleeping sinners,
into the prayers of kneeling saints,
into the pearl of clear, sweet rain.

What can the light bring?
Fade and fever, a gauche
sheen of paint,
a mirror of ourselves,
the raw burn on the edge of the horizon,
the blinding claw in the eye of desire.
Love walks through the black door
in the shade of peace.

Every brush and nib and trowel dips
for its colour in theheartof the Old Dark.
There is less of himevery year: that old grandfather dark,
revealed under the sniping beaks of drills,
pulled struggling from the quiet underbelly of the earth
he crouches under his warding hands,
he crouches into himself with shivering hands
and watches the stain of the sun
dissolve the lines of his fingers.

When he is gone, there will never be
another night as ancient as the hot breath
in the throat of a dragon, nor thick
as the flame in the core of coal and
the gangle children of the Old Dark
will crumple themselves in constant retreat,
seeking asylum in the curl of a leaf,
diminishing to a grey tatter
under the burning, pitiless sun.

The Old Dark was rucked like a rug when time began,
billowed to the edge of everything.
He learnt himself in the long retreat of stars,
gentle and patient,
knowing that even the stars burn out,
even infinity has its collapsing edge
and casts a long shadow.

The Old Dark held the father's hand
as long as he could above the child,
that night and every other,
but the glint in a bottle of barley,
and the spark in a bottle of grapes ebbs slowly.
There is nothing evil in the dark
that is not brought there, creeping, from the light.

Laura Polley

SYMBIOTIC

My young sister sits among rolled-up
canvases, ivory against white, bones
scrolled up tight. She looks hollow

as a cactus. We sit on a floor
the color of desert, scattered grains
of paint sifting twilight. Bleak stars.

As always, our talking is guarded
by art, the only conversation that fits
both frames. Perhaps it is heatstroke

or turpentine that sways me, blithe
with a waxing of clever ideas. I get
carried away, compare art to a building.

Adobe, made of mud, turning dust
into function. She listens, steady eyes
above a slanted smile. I think she is thirsty

for more metaphor, but in trying too hard
to make something of nothing I don't see
the switchback rattle in her jaw.

She punctures the air with wishbone
arms, dune-scarred wrists, and cracks
my mirage: "*My* art is negation. Making sense

of what's left." She leans back and the desert's
just a room among rooms. Fifteen years
between us at the watering hole.

I have led her to drink. I have put my little bird
on her back, navigator and scourge.

Yvonne Reddick

MUIRBURN

My father weighed a little less than at birth.
I carried him in both hands to the pines
as October brought the burning season.

When I unscrewed the urn, bone-chaff and grit
streamed out, with their gunpowder smell.
I remembered the sulphur hiss of the match—

how he taught me to breathe on the steeple of logs
until the kindling caught and flames quickened.

Cinders. Potash. Mercury.

That night, as I slept, I saw again the forest clearing
by the moor's edge, and the ring of ashes.

A skirl of smoke began to rise—
bracken curling, a fume of blaeberry leaves.
Ants broke their ranks to scatter and flee,

and a moth spun ahead of the fire-wind.
I took the path over the heath at a run.

Lead. Arsenic. Carbon monoxide.

To these elementals, we return.
A voice at my shoulder said, "You'll inherit fire."
And through the smoke I glimpsed a line of figures

on the hillside, beating and beating the heather
as the fire-front roared towards them.
A volley of shouts—"Keep the wind at your back!"

Calcium. Lithium. Carbon dioxide.

My grandmother threshing with a fire-broom,
Dad hacking a firebreak. My stillborn brother, now grown,

sprinting for the hollow where the spring once flowed—
the whole hill flaring in the updraft.

And there: a girl, running for the riverside.
She wore my face, the shade of ash.

Lois Roma-Deeley

WHY MOON JELLYFISH WON'T SPEAK OF CANCER

I suppose I should start slowly,
work up to it, draw you in,
tell you a smart story
about a wolf limping down a country lane
and how the animal is chained to a gray bearded beggar
who is toothless but properly kind
and how they're suddenly overtaken by a wind
so powerful
it blows them both clear across the ocean
where they are trapped forever on an island you never dreamed of
but fear might actually exist.
But that won't do,

it won't tell you how the words
"cancer" and "I have" take on a life all their own.
This tale won't take you to that elsewhere place
where time creates a silky pocket
and shoe-horns you inside its pouch
or how you'll press fingertips to the wall
of that translucent membrane
which divides the *just-you* from the *just-world.*
Perhaps if I mouth the words

"we are not alone"
to the trembling moon jellies glowing in the dark,
floating to the surface of an eternal sea garden,
their luminescent hearts would sing out to me
there is language beyond language—
would the sting shock you?
would you believe me then?
if I said I am always afraid now
of beginning this kind of story.

Marjorie Saiser

IN THE TIME OF THE GREAT FORGETTERS

A person could still, by wanting it,
become an animal but you had to
give up words.
You'd still have growling, like the tiger,
you'd still have warble, like the wren.
I wanted to be a snake
and slide into slits in houses,
come up in the spaces
above ceilings or between floors
and flatten there a while
or curl into a circle and wait.
I knew a woman who would
talk to me if I slid out an inch or two
onto her porch. *Come on,* she'd say.
In or out, she'd say. And I'd choose
out. I'd slide onto the boards
of her porch, and rest. She'd remark
on easy things, the heat of the sun
or the phase of the moon, she'd call me
Racer. And when she got tired,
she'd go inside. I'd lift myself
rib by rib and coil up into the chair
she'd left, her body heat still
there in the cushions. I was despised
in those days, like now,
but I found a warm depression,
almost a lap, a little valley that I
fit into. I had given up words,
my soundless tongue flicking in air,
but I take words back again
now and then. I make a trade
so I can tell you this, and see
if you forget or remember.

Anne Sandor

OSSUARIES

In Greece where arable land is scarce
and cremation a sin, they dig up their dead
after three years, wash the bones in wine,
say the ritual prayers, file them in boxes
in the *koxalothoxion*, the bone-house.

The Choctaw leave their dead
to the elements on covered platforms
before sending in the bone pickers, tattooed
in honor of their work, who gather the bones,
use their long-nailed fingers to pick them clean.

In the Czech ossuary of Sedlec, a chandelier
of bone lights the nave, garlands of skulls
festoon vaulted arches, the handiwork
of crafty monks honoring the congregants
who rested briefly in soil from the Holy Land.

In Cologne, bone mosaics in cross-hatch patterns
adorn the walls of the Golden Chamber,
the reliquary of St. Ursula and her 11,000 virgins
slaughtered by the Huns, whose supplicants wrote
across the field of bone: "Holy Ursula, Pray For Us."

As Paris grew, they dug up their dead,
stacked their crisscrossed femurs,
skulls cheek to cheek, sorted by cemetery,
and for a small fee, you can visit them
in the catacombs under the suburban sprawl.

When my son was small he asked
to be left in a cave when he died
so animals could come and feast
and when they were done,
they would scatter his bones in the forest.

I will return to nature, he told me, bright-eyed
at the prospect, as the mother in me thought
no—I will gather your bones, wash them in wine,
pick them clean, adorn the walls with your lovely, long femurs,
fashion mosaics with the fine bones of your hands and feet.

I would build him an ossuary, keep him close,
but my hands cupping his skull, his newly shorn hair,
his face shining proudly only inches from mine—
I thought better of it and praised instead his wisdom,
how great his place in the world, his generous spirit.

Joyce Schmid

PHONE CALLS

I dreamed that you were calling me
and calling me, I couldn't make you stop,
and then I woke up to the telephone—
you calling me.

I wish I could have smiled, and said
good morning to the pieces I have left of you
my little sister, how I wish I could be
only kind to you.

When we were little, I would ditch you,
clingy child, but I regretted it
when we were grown. We spoke so often
on the phone, my children brandished scissors

threatening to cut the line.
You were so gentle with our mother
as she died, drinking as you always did
the acid of her tears.

Today, you clutch at me in panic
as your world unties, and now, again,
I find I want to run from you,
your pleading eyes.

Mark Scott

LOVE POEM

Let me count the ways in which one of us could suddenly lose interest:

1. By sheer willpower.
2. By taking shears to the other's hair.
3. By being a bear, who's primary interest is salmon and streams.
4. The paleo diet.
5. Stealing my socks without permission.
6. Poisoning me with arsenic.
7. Peanut allergies.
8. Not thinking George Washington Carver is important and should be remembered.
9. No longer believing in the power of vaccination.
10. Building my house with asbestos and not telling me.
11. Moving into a cabin in the woods to write a book about a pond without telling me.
12. Being too similar to the other's other significant other.
13. If Death did us part.
14. If I did the Cupid Shuffle every wedding we went to.
15. If you found me drunk when I told you I'd quit.
16. If I catch the kitchen on fire one more time you swear to God.
17. If I told you with my straight face I don't know God. or Jesus.
18. By needing space.
19. By it not being you, but me.
20. Finding someone else, someone that's:
21. Better looking.
22. Better smelling.
23. Better in bed, etc.
24. Softer-headed.
25. Or shallow.
26. Whatever makes us feel better than we do alone.
27. Becoming someone else, someone that:
28. No longer identifies as a member of the human race, feels entirely extra-terrestrial and doesn't understand what the other says when they speak to them.

29. Comes up with bizarre excuses like the one above as some sort of non-sequitur justification/humorous defense in response to the accusation of ignoring what the other says when they speak to them.
30. Actively diminishes the liberties of marginalized groups.
31. Actively makes the other feel like a marginalized group or, adversely, the diminisher thereof.
32. Enjoys pineapple on pizza, or in another's case, is too passionate about their hatred of such.
33. Pokes holes in condoms.
34. Identifies as vegan.
35. Doesn't like roller-coasters (actual roller-coasters).
36. Identifies as carnivore.
37. Lets friends text/sext/drive drunk.
38. Identifies as the sun or the moon or something as equally impractical, unreachable.
39. We grow old together. So old we lose both sight and hearing, stumbling around whatever dome we inhabit, avoiding sharp objects and barely made aware of the others presence.
40. We slowly grow apart, both of us being seashores.
41. One of us exhibits some morbid fascination with seashells everytime The Police come on the radio.
42. Neither of us do anything but pay strict and close attention to one another.
43. Neither of us likes the other's poetry anymore.
44. Both of us audition for leads in a play by Tennessee Williams.
45. Or Lawrence Ferlinghetti.
46. One of us carries a tape-worm reaching critical mass, which makes us act out in all sorts of weird ways, all while being dangerously and unfunctionally bloated.
47. One of us carries our child.
48. One of us is Zeus, post-coitus.
49. If I was Zeus, made you my heifer, and gifted you to my very angry wife.
50. If our love was the heifer Zeus made out of Io, the priestess, and we were Io's father who—in someone elses story—looks at the river with regret and feigning forgetfulness turns away.

Heidi Seaborn

DRESS UP

~a ghazal

Blooming rose, nipped and held like a promise in my womb,
I gathered bouquets of pink-lavender-gingham-piped-polka-dotted dresses.

Folded, layered in tissue, they waited for your fat fists to slide through tulip sleeves,
your furry little head to pop peek-a-boo through the peter pan-collared dresses.

Light snow, New York City, Upper Eastside children's shop—in the window,
a silk-taffeta-poinsettia-swirl-big-back-bow-smocked-bodice dress.

I flew it home in a box. You wore shiny patent Mary Janes, delicate snowbell
socks with your kindergarten-Christmas-pageant-skirt-twirling-dancing dress.

The flower girl flowing down the aisle, a crown of rosebuds, ribbons
down your shoulders, kissing the back of your sea-green-tulle dress.

Sixteen in the once-mine-then-your-midnight-silk-organza-nestled-under-peach-
blossom-shoulders-prom dress. At the gate, you turned, lifted your chin, eyes addressed

this moment of wearing a dress, wearing a boy's gardenia, wearing me,
wearing this skin to play the part I'd given you in our game of dress up.

Crumpled, stashed out of sight, in the back of the closet, my last gift to you dress—
slinky-silk-tie-dyed-fuschia-lime-green-teal-yellow-down-to-your-ankles dress.

I saw you in it—all hippy chicky—then saw your look,
saw your face close, a morning glory at night, as you slipped on that dress,

saw how it wore on you, left lush lilac bruises like the tattoos
that would one day cover you—art inscribed over wounds dressed.

Secrets wound round like wisteria—until the petals fell.
Oh, I see you now as born my beautiful daughter—adored, undressed.

Kurt Steinwand

OCCUPATION

At the factory gate a sergeant-major sits at a foldable table. He wears a swastika on his arm, and a civil servant with the same symbol holds a stack of papers that flutter like doves trying to take wing. Not by wind, but trucks rumbling past and the air sucked up, following. Exhaustion. The citizens look gassed.

Occupation? The man is careful not to say artist or teacher. Draftsman, he says with Polish pride. I can draw battlefields, these city streets. The sergeant-major over his shoulder: Zeichner, and it gets written into the doves.

Occupation? The man pushes up a teenager in a wheelchair. Smile, he whispers, and the young man smiles all teeth and gums. This is my son. He is a timekeeper. Accurate to the second. Go ahead, test him.

The sergeant-major stares back. The father trips over his own tongue, trying to persuade: and dishwasher. He can go all day. Never chafes. The sergeant-major over his shoulder: Geschirrspüler, as the other holds tightly to the doves.

That's right. The father points at the papers, 'Gesher-spooler'. Write it down. He imitates the writing, the stamping.

Can the child speak for himself?

Of course. Certainly. Excuse me. Speak, my boy. I mean, young man. You're nearly a man,

so the son asks, What kind of car do you drive? The two men look at each other as the doves blow wild, trying to break free.

We all drive Mercedes, says the sergeant-major with a snort as he stamps one of the books, hands it back. Laughter, such a strange echo among the exhaust and din of the city.

They follow two soldiers shouldering rifles. The
sergeant-major calls after them:

I hope you like trucks. More laughter. We have many trucks. And
tanks on the way! A flock of pigeons explodes from a ledge.

A soldier blocks the father with his rifle. The other takes
over pushing his son along the dirt lot where the trucks
idle, mufflers like in a cabaret full of smokers.

He is rolled further into the distance. Mist diffuses. Engines
rev. Gears catch. A ringing fills the man's ears.

I'll be right there, my boy, he shouts.

What is this? he asks, confronting the soldier.
That's my son. He relies on me.

With Lugers troops shoot pigeons from the sky.

A ramp is pulled, and the other rolls his boy up into the payload
filled with children. He tilts the chair, shakes it like emptying
a bag. His son falls out, starts to cry in a cold drizzle.

The soldier pushes the empty chair, mud collected
on its wheels, disappears behind a tent.

His boy reaches through the truck's wood slats, calls for
him. A blur, but it is him. His father knows the terrified
screams, their legs as useless as wings in a cage.

Sophia Stid

THE MARRIAGE BED

for Julia

We dragged our beds outside & pushed them together
on the porch that summer we lived & worked in the woods,
& we slept there under heavy blankets beneath the cedar trees
in the cold high Sierra nights & laughing, called it the marriage bed—

sometimes stumbling to bed happy & drunk from the bonfires
we lit by the river, the fires where you sang
this is my body, take and destroy it, if you please
while we were learning something different—& because

we walked home through the meadow, there were seeds
in the seams of our jeans, which we shimmied out of to sleep—
too tired to take off our shirts & bras & when we woke
our bare legs were cold & sometimes I'd find your hand

in my hair, which was long then—our jeans an alphabet
on the floorboards, dirty tangled language of the days where
we were learning how to be real & hungry, how to eat
the nights, we'd sneak into the restaurant where we waited tables

& raid the walk-in fridge, shaking cinnamon-sugar over sour-
dough toast shining with butter, burnt crusts brittle, smoky
from the broken toaster, somehow that bite between my back teeth
always exact & what I wanted—we ate on the line, barefoot,

sitting on the counter swinging our legs, holding tomatoes
like apples up to our mouths, taking big cartoon bites, quiver-silk
of seeds slaking down our wrists all held yellow in liquid space,
next the avocadoes I ate with so much flaked salt you said

I'd die overnight from thirst & so I drank long draughts
of cold creek water from a jar & listen: there was always
dirt in it & listen: I didn't care, there was also mint
& that whole summer I never felt thirsty, we were always

standing on hot rocks high over the American River &
holding hands & saying *okay* & jumping into muscled water
& sometimes we stood so still in the riverbed
that fish swam iridescent into us, tracing our ankles

silver—that summer we learned to walk in the dark
without a light, our muscles were quick & strong & female
& always slightly flexed & we slept in the marriage bed,
where a part of me, still, is always resting—& years after,

you wrote to me, *you were the first woman I had ever wanted*
to be & with that bed we made an enormous space
for each other into which we will always be rising—
yours the only other body I know as well as my mother's—

the bodies of the women that made me ready for my life.

Allen Sweat

RIDING THE DREAM

Last month in Fort Worth I saw a girl fly
out of the Himalaya, slap her head
on the back wall, die right there as Prince played
Purple Rain. They said a lap bar cotter
pin the size of a paper clip broke.
All I know is Earl got fired on the spot.

I grab a section of track still frozen
to a Dubuque County corn stalk reminding
me there's eight towns to go before winter's
end. The new guy stands in the field, breath
fogging moonlight, holding a wrench and floppy
cardboard box piled with greasy bolts.

Everything has a place, must fit perfectly,
I tell him. Kids' lives are riding on
The Dream Machine. This coaster's got to cling
securely to icy tracks looping the
moon, dodging stars, 'til my flip of the switch
sends them off running, eyes bright with spinning
Fireballs, gyrating Gravitrons, hand
in their sweet baby's rear blue jean pocket
palming their Mommy's twenty dollar bill.

Remember kid, for them life is all out
front. They will not see the old Ring Toss
operator shooting up behind the
curtain or the fourteen year old getting
pregnant in a back row porta-potty.
No worries under rainbow lights.

There's no way they'll understand a high school
drop out, fresh from the memory of his
parent's plucked from a semi-truck flattened
station wagon, working Balloon Darts
to save the farm. Let's get this finished, I'm
looking forward to a warm cup of bourbon.

And who knows, maybe tonight the couple
in the photo glued to my camper ceiling
will swirl with me down dusty back roads
to find a little patch of hardened clay, once
fertile enough to build an American Dream.

Barbara Ungar

THE LAST JAGUAR

(Panthera onca)

The Jaguar God of the Night Lord of the Underworld.

The last jaguar in Texas shot in 1948, the last female
jaguar in the US shot the same year as JFK.

Schoolkids in Tuscon named the last jaguar standing
El Jefe The Boss. He prowls the Santa Rita Mountains
an immigrant from the Sierra Madre.

The last jaguar before him Macho B lured with
female scat killed in a botch-job in 2009.

Two centuries ago Thomas Jefferson recorded
the jaguar an American animal.

Two thousand centuries ago jaguars came from Asia when
dire wolves saber-toothed cats and mammoths roamed.

Two hundred centuries ago people followed
them across the Bering Land Bridge.

In Mexican Spanish the jaguar is el tigre. Jaguar comes
from the native yaguar he who kills with one leap.

Peerless at ambush, jaguars bite through skulls, leap into water
onto crocodiles haul cows up trees. Jaguars avoid & rarely attack
us unlike their old-world relations—leopards, lions, tigers.

Solitary. Elusive. Their rosettes help them
disappear in dappled deep-forest light.

Hard to spot let alone count.

El Jefe can be known by his unique coat.

Where jaguars once roamed the southwest freely El Jefe hunts
alone. The Wall will keep females out, making El Jefe the very last.

The Ese Ejja People of the Amazon say The Jaguar only
shows himself to you when you are ready to see him.

John Sibley Williams

IT'S ONLY AN ISLAND IF YOU LOOK AT IT FROM THE WATER

—after Martin Brody

I'm just as terrified by what I've chosen
to surround myself with. Not the swells
& surf, riptides, teeth, the arcane eons
implied by all that cold Atlantic blue.
Mine's more a forest—slashed, burned.
Friends. An unhealthy reliance on storm-
lit fields, the kind the lightning loves
more than metal or water. Cigarettes.
Black-lunged stars. The maps of muscle
bulging from a horse's croup. Pretending
I can read them. My mother's ghost, held
closer now that she cannot be held. If it's true
what I touch touches me back, I'll run my
hands along every musket hole in every Civil
War-era farmhouse until I feel what it's like
to kill my brother over another's servitude.
There never were any undiscovered countries.
The sea runs north to south to Midwest
to maw. Sawgrass grows long as oars. Oars
bone-clean, hospital-white, jutting
up from all this green like unused silos.
Chief, I understand that breathing here
among so many dead suggests a debt
we spend our whole lives asking how
best to pay off. Our only currency: labored
love. Letting our sons play at drowning
in that rickety rowboat surrounded by
our fears. Walking freely into that open mouth
with both eyes open—daring the world to swallow.

Jim Glenn Thatcher

THE DRUNKEN NOVEL

Himself the novel wanting to be its novelist.
Living it, suffering it, writing it, but never building the book.
Derelict words by a drunken writer in a staggering scrawl
across one first page endlessly abandoned to another.
The beginning unending and never beginning.
The protagonist become his own incessant antagonist—
gifted in words but lost in discipline.—The pages delirious,
stumbling, wandering—nothing but notes, fragments, paragraphs—
some brilliant, but none settling into a story—its idea elusive,
ever-changing.—Every moment another metaphor,
every day another allegory—their meanings his meanings
but overwhelmed and entangled, dragging him down
into the ever-darkening maze.—Beer blackening his being.—
His own first person anguishing in its poisoning—
all day every day through all those years
every cell in his body screaming in withdrawal—
all night every night drunk again; the agon of agony
from that dark attic in Bethlehem through all the ensuing hovels
and rubbles, all the labor and factory jobs that followed.
Physical addiction validated by moral obligation—
He thought he needed suffering— The Authenticity of Tragedy—
Was he not living it? The Sisyphus of Six-packs?
The Tortured Hero proud to be deluded in his delusions?—
The Great Novel of the Western World?—To someday
be recognized as worthy of his tradition—Dostoevsky,
Hesse, Knut Hamsun, Conrad, Kafka, *Heinrich Muller*—
Apostates all, attitudes and atmospheres matching his own wanderings—
That negative apartment on Positively 4th Street—cockroaches
swimming in his tea, crawling through his rice...
The abandoned MA thesis—Freud and the Philosophy of History,
itself evaporating before the novel, undone, studied but not written,
obsessed over—pages begun and fallen away,
adrift in the litter of the lost literature of his own lost lifetime.

Years and scrawlings carrying him on, sketching his situations—
the Time Farm in Pennsylvania— Settled there by old friends.
Like him, all ex-history students. Horses, guns, drugs. Stoned.
Riding out into the fields of night, each in his own century—
his the 19th—Russia—*Holy Mother Russ*—then back every day
to his job in the hangover factory.—The year in Greece—
The lover of ruins ruined himself and knowing it.
Astray across Crete, angst in every pen scratch. Then coming
back to hole up for three winters in that abandoned farm
outside of Circleville, what was left of the house slowly
caving in around him. Snakes in summer sliding up
between the floorboards, winter coming in through the holes.
The pen hapless in his hand. Decades pass, the novel long dead,
entombed in the marbled covers of abandoned notebooks—

Let them lie there. That history now his strength.
His life still literature. He has risen from regret.
The 'fragments' he now writes not fragments but poems—
They carry their full meaning.

Jim Glenn Thatcher

WAITING FOR PERSEPHONE

It is March. Late March. The drag end of March,
scraping like an anchor across the bottoms of his brain-pan.
The slowest season in the slow-turning calendar of his years.
The persistence of rotting snow, the raw mockery
of a gray sun, of hard winds driven from a bitter sky.
Every year he does what he promises himself he won't do:
Suffers the last meanness of winter like an adolescent
craving the still-distant delights of first love.
Leans into Spring with the full weight of his heart.
Strains to lever life upward from the frozen mud,
the long tilt of the planet. Breathes on the tinder
of longing like the colas in his stove.
Listens for the gutter of time in every thawing rivulet.
Watches for the signs: The droop of catkins
forming in the aspens, the red haze
gathering in the maples,
a deepening blush in the birch-tops.
He wants to sleep, to hoard the changes
like fluids in his body.
To dream past the distance of April,
the crowns of skunk cabbage
rising from brown litters,
the chorused curl of fiddleheads,
the thick throw of bluets at the meadow's edge—
To wake at last to the green trumpets of fullness,
their lush treasures overflowing an emerald world.

Keith Woodruff

HOT MESS

i

Because your eyes never
became the color they'd be.

A dry mouth, dead birds
fixed against the sky.
Every fall the flowers
say no, and yet.

We give clocks
human features—
hands face—
but nothing
from our hot insides,
and no one ever says
the trains roaring
past the station
sound like tornadoes.

Unhappy with my life's
lack of absolute despair,
I keep moving my house
to wherever the rain
is falling.

ii

Memo: two months into hyper-mourning, I am no longer able to add value at work beyond a dimensional PowerPoint. I get a letter draft that I can't "plus up". My brand takes a hit. Beggared by our grief we droop like sunflowers, heavy-headed, into late September. The goldfinches that deface us, the only color we have. Everyone scribbles in a purple card ... *thinking of you, in our prayers*, confirming also the death of words, handwriting, *et al.*

iii

I stare like a scientist into my gin.
Then a moon, then a sun, and us
that agonizing cry in between.

Bracha Sharp

WORDS

Mostly,
Come sleep,
I am words.

While sleeping, or eating, or singing,
Words fill me up like rainwater on the deck.

They come, dripping through me like rain
Through wooden slats, like sap — sate me
Like a prayer.

I sip words, imbibe them like green tea,

And always, a poem is forming beneath
The surface,
Frothing up,
Surfacing green and raw, like the wet,
Leaden trees after rain.

Who knows why one person is filled
With them and will pant like a sweaty dog,
Until their message is released,
Let loose to flow?

Always, I am the fullness and the
Ache of words,

Sometimes,
The cavern
Where words do not flow,

And in that pause, there is the round
Fullness of music and the slow, methodical
Dance or the frenzied reconstruction of the
Words, out of hibernation.

Still, I am inside of them and out,

And always, I am listening—
For the songs that they sing,
For the wait between the
Fierce, lonely hollow
To be filled

And my next step.

Victoria Richards

WEANING

It's 01.20 in the morning and you're awake
awake
awake
I offer you my breasts but you don't want them,
which makes me feel strange and redundant.
We struggle in each other's arms as you twist
and writhe, reel backwards, lead me in a stilted dance
across the carpet, the sea-green carpet, which
is also the ocean floor, bumping against the shipwreck
of your cot, dragging us under. The
bubble-wrap tentacles of an octopus wave
mournfully from the ceiling, clashing
against our iron weight.
Your gull cry pierces the night. You are
angry with me. You point at the door, "da da da",
as my milk chokes in your throat.
What more do I have to give you?
Not my heart, you already have it.
They ripped it out of my chest when you were born,
grafted it to your back with paste and a palette knife
while they stitched me back together.
It bleeds openly, that's why you sleep
on your front, even though you're not
supposed to, because of SIDS. In
the mornings your sheets are sodden red,
and so is your hair, my blonde, bloodied, darling boy.
You wouldn't like my tears—they
only fall in small, dark spaces, when
I read something sad on my phone
about lions or kids getting killed in America.
Take my mind—you're welcome to it, though
it is broken, so you might not enjoy it much.
I left it behind at an 18-course tasting menu at the

Dorchester, layers on layers on stark, white plates.
There was foam and something called a velouté
that we paid £180 for, so we pretended to love it,
called it "rich and complex", narrowed
our eyes and nodded. I'm not sure I even liked it,
it left a strange, sour taste in my mouth, but—
I don't know what else to feed you.

NOTES ON CONTRIBUTORS

Kemmer Anderson, poet, taught English for 40 years at McCallie School in Chattanooga, Tennessee, where he was Amnesty International Chapter advisor and B-team soccer coach. A veteran of U.S. Army in Korea and traveler in Greece, Palestine and Israel, he received N.E.H. grants on Milton, Galileo, Thucydides. A graduate of Davidson College, he has received a M.A. in English from UT-Chattanooga and M.A. degree in humanities from St. John's College, Annapolis. He has published 10 chapbooks and 3 poetry books: Wing Shadows Over Walden Ridge, Songs of Bethlehem: Nativity Poems, and Palamedes: The Lost Muse of Justice. He and his wife Martha lived and gardened on Wing Shadow Farm for 21 years.

Alice Ashe's previous publications: *Sixfold* Summer 2017 Poetry - "lilith" & other poems. Upcoming publications: *december* magazine Fall/Winter 2018 - "What the Wildflowers Get"

Jacqueline Berger teaches writing at Notre Dame de Namur University in Belmont, California. Her fourth book, *The Day You Miss Your Exit*, was published by Broadstone Books this year. Previous books include *The Gift That Arrives Broken*, winner of the 2010 Autumn House Poetry Prize,

Things That Burn, selected by Mark Strand as the 2004 winner of the Agha Shahid Ali Prize, and *The Mythologies of Danger*, winner of the 1998 Bluestem Award and the Bay Area Book Awards (now the Northern California Book Awards) Poetry Prize. Several of my poems have been featured on Garrison Keillor's *Writers Almanac* as well as in numerous anthologies and journals, including *The Iowa Review, American Poetry: The Next Generation, On The Verge, Old Dominion Review, Rhino, River Styx*, and *Nimrod*.

F. J. Bergmann edits poetry for *Mobius: The Journal of Social Change* (mobiusmagazine.com), and imagines tragedies on or near exoplanets. Work appears irregularly in *Analog, Asimov's, Polu Texni, Pulp Literature, Silver Blade*, and other places. *A Catalogue of the Further Suns* won the 2017 Gold Line Press poetry chapbook contest.

Sarah Blanchard has recently returned to writing poetry and short fiction after spending several decades as a business teacher, corporate marketer, non-fiction writer, and facility manager for an astronomical observatory in Hawai'i. Several of her early poems were published in *Calyx, Welter, Conscience, The Planetary Report*, and *The Red Fox Review*. She currently works as a real estate agent and lives in Raleigh, NC, with her husband, three horses, three dogs and several chickens.

Eleanor Bluestein lives in Southern California. She is the author of *Tea and Other Ayama Na Tales*, a collection of linked stories inspired by travels in Southeast Asia. She is completing a novel (*Slumming*) and a short story collection (*Louder than Words*).

Constance Campana has been published in various journals and small press magazines, including *Dogwood, Three Rivers Poetry Journal, 491 Magazine, Brown Journal of the Arts, Cleaver,* and *SNReview*. She has also twice won the American Academy of Poets award and the Enthwhistle Prize for poetry and fiction. Constance grew up in Kentucky, but after receiving her MFA from Brown University, she stayed in Rhode Island and recently moved to Massachusetts, where she teaches writing at Wheaton College.

Shuyu Cao is a poet and filmmaker based in Los Angeles, CA. She was born in China and grew up in Chapel Hill, North Carolina. After graduating from Davidson College with a BA in English, she made her way out west to explore new storytelling mediums.

J.L. Cooper received the Tupelo Quarterly Prose Open Prize, TQ9, judged by Pulitzer winner Adam Johnson. Additional awards are First Place in Short Short Fiction in *New Millennium Writings*, 2013, Second Place in Essay in *Literal Latte*, 2014, and First Runner-up for the 2016 nonfiction prize in *StoryQuarterly*. His full-length book of poetry, *An Ocean Large Enough* (WordTech Communications) is available on Amazon Books. His short stories, poetry and a craft piece have appeared in numerous journals including *The Manhattan Review, Oberon Poetry Magazine, Hippocampus, Leveler, The Tishman Review, 3Elements Review, Structo, The Sun* (Reader's Write), and in other journals and anthologies. jlcooper.net

Jack Cooper is author of the poetry collection *Across My Silence* (World Audience, Inc., 2007). His poetry, flash fiction, and mini-plays have appeared in *Rattle, Slant, Slab, Bryant*

Literary Review, The Main Street Rag, North American Review, and others. His poetry has also been selected for Ted Kooser's "American Life in Poetry" and Tweetspeak's Every Day Poems. His play *That Perfect Moment*, co-written with Charles Bartlett, was a headliner at the NOHO Arts Center in North Hollywood, California, and The Little Victory in the 2009-10 seasons. He is co-editor of www.KYSOflash.com.

Patrick Dawson spent nearly three decades as a journalist, most of it as an award-winning national and international correspondent for NBC News, CNN, and ABC. He is currently at work on a collection of short fiction and a novel. He lives in London and New York.

Lisa Dordal (M.Div., M.F.A.) is a Pushcart Prize nominated poet whose work has appeared in numerous journals and anthologies including *Best New Poets, Ninth Letter, Cave Wall, CALYX, The Greensboro Review, Vinyl Poetry* and *Nasty Women Poets: An Unapologetic Anthology of Subversive Verse*. She is the recipient of an Academy of American Poets Prize, the Robert Watson Poetry Prize, and the Betty Gabehart Poetry Prize. She teaches in the English Department at Vanderbilt University and her first full-length collection of poetry, *Mosaic of the Dark*, is available from Black Lawrence Press. lisadordal.com

C.W. Emerson's work has appeared or is forthcoming in journals including *Atlanta Review, Crab Orchard Review, december, Greensboro Review, The American Journal of Poetry, New Ohio Review* and others. Emerson was a finalist for the 2018 New Millennium Award for Poetry, the 2018 New Ohio Review Poetry Contest, the 2017 Two Sylvias Chapbook Prize, and the 2017 New Letters Prize for Poetry.

He lives in Palm Springs, California where he works as a clinical psychologist.

Robert Evory is the Assistant Coordinator of the Creative Writing Department at Western Michigan University where he is Doctoral Assistant. He is the Managing Editor and co-founder of *The Poet's Billow*. He has an MFA from Syracuse University. His poetry is featured or is forthcoming in: *Georgia Review, Spillway, Spoon River Review, Natural Bridge, The Fat City Review, Nashville Review, Wisconsin Review, Arroyo, The Madison Review, Water~Stone Review*, and elsewhere. thepoetsbillow.org

Robert Evory's manuscript *The Failure of My Music* was a finalist for the University of Akron Press, Tupelo Press, 42 Miles Press, and the New Issues Press Poetry Prize and his chapbook *Day Today* was a semifinalist for Yes Yes Books and the Fine Arts Work Center. His poems have also received recognition from the *Georgia Review, Pudding House Publishing*, Cutbank Big Fish Prose Poetry Contest, and the Summer Literary Seminars. He has received grants from the Prague Summer Seminars, Syracuse University, Vermont Writing Studio, The Pop Culture Conference, and others.

Ed Frankel divides his time between Sonoma County in Northern California and Los Angeles where he teaches at UCLA and for Antioch University Los Angeles BA and MFA programs. His poems have appeared in numerous journals and he has published two chapbooks: *When the Catfish are in Bloom: Requiem For John Fahey* and *People of the Air*, which won the New American Chapbook prize in 2008. He won first place prizes and awards in the 2015 *Dogwood Journal of Poetry and Prose Competition*, The 2010 Little

Red Tree International Poetry Competition, the 2009 New Millennium Poetry Competition, the 2006 Winning Writers War Poetry competition, the *Hackney* National Poetry competition 2006, and the 2003 *Confluence* Poetry competition. He was nominated three times for the *Pushcart Best of the Small Presses* Poetry Prize and the California Book Award and was invited to read at the Strokestown International Poetry festival in Ireland.

Sam Griswold is a professor of Italian at Mercy College and a writer/translator some of the time.

Alyson Hagy is the author of eight works of fiction, including the forthcoming novel *Scribe* (Graywolf Press). Her flash fiction has most recently been published in *INCH* and *Kenyon Review* (online). She lives in Laramie, Wyoming.

Michele Harris was awarded the Paul G. Zolbrod prize and, more recently, the David A. Kennedy prize in the field of poetry. Her work has appeared in *Anderbo, The Prose-Poem Project, Dirtflask, Cicada, Eclectica, Escarp, Stirring*, and elsewhere. Currently, she works at MIT and holds an MFA in Creative Writing from the University of Massachusetts Boston, where she teaches for the Osher Lifelong Learning Institute.

Elizabeth Jackson is a practicing psychologist with writing published across a variety of fields, including the social sciences, the visual and literary arts. My poems have appeared in anthologies and journals, including *Crab Orchard Review, LUMINA, Poet Lore*, and *The Southern Poetry Anthology: North Carolina*. In January 2018, Plan B Press published my chapbook, *River of Monuments*.

Trish Lindsey Jaggers' "Crazy-Eights" goal as a poet is to, "Create simply: Write so an eight-year-old can read it, an eighteen-year-old can understand it, and an eighty-year-old will have lived it." The author of *Holonym: poems* (FLP, 2016), Jaggers teaches English and creative writing at Western Kentucky University..

AKaiser is member of the poetry collective Sweet Action and contributor to its chapbooks, *My Mother is a Tardigrade*, created for a www.350.org benefit, 2018; *Sampler,* published for the 2017 Governors Island Poetry Festival; and *Buried Paths,* donated to a Standing Rock benefit (2016). You can also read her work in *Amsterdam Quarterly, Crosswinds Poetry Journal, Manzano Mountain Review, ROAR, Temenos* and *Wasafiri*. She participated in Tupelo Press's 30/30 Project in 2016. Her poem, *The Sound of Clothes,* is the Sow's Ear Poetry Journal 2017 poetry prize winner.

Kristin Kostick is a poetry and nonfiction writer currently working on a collection of essays called *You Not You* about the advantages of self-deception. She is also a medical anthropologist researching bioethics and health policy at Baylor College of Medicine in Houston. kristinkostick.com

Sandy Longley is an Associate Professor of English of English at Columbia-Greene Community College. Her collection of poems called *Navigating the Waters* was published in 2016 by Finishing Line Press.

Dr. Barbara Mossberg, President Emerita Goddard College, Poet in Residence Pacific Grove (CA), humanities activist, dramaturg, playwright, actor, literary critic, and professor (California State University and University of Oregon), founded and hosts weekly Poetry Slow Down (podcast BarbaraMossberg.com) and lectures worldwide on poetry, including as Fulbrighter and former U.S. Scholar in Residence (USIA).

Terri Niccum lives in Southern California where she is an advocate for children with special needs. She was selected as a semi-finalist for the 2014 Pablo Neruda Prize for Poetry. Her chapbook, *Looking Snow in the Eye*, was released in 2015 by Finishing Line Press. Her poems have appeared in *Cadence Collective* and in the *Incandescent Mind* anthologies, *Volume 2* and *Selfish Work*. Her work has also been featured in *The Poeming Pigeon* anthologies, *From the Garden* and *Love Poems; Nimrod International Journal; The Maine Review; 1932 Quarterly Review; Literary Orphans; Angel City Review*; and *Pretty Owl Poetry*. She loves live music and is learning to identify birds by their songs.

Damen O'Brien is a Queensland poet. Damen was joint winner of the Peter Porter Poetry Prize and has won the Yeats Poetry Prize, the KSP Poetry Award and the Ipswich Poetry Festival, and was shortlisted in the Gwen Harwood Poetry Prize, ACU Poetry Prize, Val Vallis Award, Newcastle Poetry Prize, and Martha Richardson Memorial Poetry Prize. Damen has previously been published in *Rabbit, Southerly, Cordite, Island, Verity La* and *StylusLit*.

Laura Polley is a poet and essayist with an MFA from Lesley University. She has published poems in *Crab Orchard Review, Margie, Salamander, Slate Online*, and other venues. Laura is rekindling her lifelong calling toward a writing career after raising three children via "regular" jobs.

Yvonne Reddick is a poet and researcher. Her pamphlet *Translating Mountains* (Seren, 2017) won the *Mslexia* Magazine Pamphlet Competition and was selected as a favourite pamphlet of the year in the *Times Literary Supplement*. Her work appears in publications such as *The Guardian, PN Review* and *The North*. She has received a Northern Writer's Award, a Hawthornden Fellowship and a place on the 2017-18 Jerwood/Arvon mentoring scheme. Her book *Ted Hughes: Environmentalist and Ecopoet* is published by Palgrave Macmillan.

Victoria Richards is a freelance journalist and writer. She has worked for *BBC News, The Times* and *The Independent* and has appeared on *Newsnight, BBC World* and *ITV News*. She was 'highly commended' for poetry in the Bridport Prize 2017, shortlisted for poetry in the Hysteria UK Writing Competition 2017 and longlisted for poetry in the Yeovil Literary Prize 2017. She has had poems published in the Bridport Prize 2017 anthology, Ellipsis Zine *One*, and forthcoming editions of *Shooter Literary Magazine* and *Hysteria 6*. She has also had flash fiction published in the *National Flash Fiction Day Anthology 2017*. She lives in London where she is working variously on a novel, short stories and a poetry collection. Twitter: @nakedvix

Lois Roma-Deeley's full-length poetry collection, *The Short List of Certainties*, won the Jacopone da Todi Poetry Book Prize, (Franciscan University Press, 2017). Her previous books include: *Rules of Hunger, northSight,* and *High Notes*, a Paterson Poetry Prize Finalist. Roma-Deeley has published widely in numerous poetry anthologies and literary journals, nationally and internationally including *Spillway, Columbia Poetry Review, North Dakota Quarterly* and many more.

Currently, she serves as Associate Editor of the poetry journal *Presence*. Roma-Deeley was named U.S. Professor of the Year, Community College, by the Carnegie Foundation for the Advancement of Teaching and CASE in 2012-2013 and is a recipient of a 2016 Arizona Commission on the Arts grant for her poetry. loisroma-deeley.com

Marsh Rose is a psychotherapist, freelance writer, and college educator living in northern California. Rose's short stories have appeared in a variety of publications in print and online. Her writing style is narrative nonfiction.

Marjorie Saiser is the author of six books of poetry and co-editor of two anthologies. Her new book, *The Woman in the Moon*, contains poems which look at ordinary things (even the moon) in a new way. Her work has been published in *American Life in Poetry, Nimrod, Rattle.com, PoetryMagazine.com, RHINO, Chattahoochee Review, Poetry East, Poet Lore*, and other journals. She has received the WILLA Award and nominations for the Pushcart Prize. poetmarge.com

Patricia Sammon was born and raised in Canada and immigrated to the United States when she was 16 years old. She studied history at Cornell University, then completed graduate school at Queen's University in Canada. Sammon has written a novel, many short stories and is working on a play.

Anne Sandor Born and raised in Brooklyn, NY, Anne Sandor earned a BA from Vassar College and an MFA in Creative Writing from Vermont College. She is an Associate Professor of English and Writing Consultancy Coordinator

at SUNY Orange in Middletown, NY, where she teaches Contemporary Novel and Creative Writing.

Joyce Schmid's recent work has appeared in *Missouri Review, Poetry Daily, New Ohio Review, Sugar House Review,* and other journals and anthologies. She lives in Palo Alto, California, with her husband of over half a century.

Mark Scott is a musician in the Dallas/Fort-Worth area and a student at the University of North Texas.

Heidi Seaborn starting writing poetry in 2016. Since then her work has appeared in over 40 journals and anthologies including *Nimrod International Journal* (2017 Pablo Neruda Prize for Poetry semi-finalist), *The New Guard* (2017 Knightville Prize semi-finalist), *Penn Review, Timberline, Gravel* (Best of Net nominee), *American Journal of Poetry,* as the political pamphlet *Body Politic* (Mount Analogue Press), on a Seattle bus and in her forthcoming chapbook *Finding My Way Home* (Finishing Line Press). She is on the editorial staff of *The Adroit Journal* and lives in Seattle. heidiseabornpoet.com

Xiao Yue (Shelly) Shan is a poet and essayist born in Dongying, China and residing in Tokyo, Japan. Her first chapbook, *How Often I Have Chosen Love*, is forthcoming by way of Frontier Poetry. Shelly haunts the internet at shellyshan.com.

Bracha Sharp has had a poem entitled, "Thinking About Basho" published in the *American Poetry Review* (November/ December, 2016, Volume 45, No. 06) and placed first in the 2016 Hackney Literary Awards in their National Poetry category. This poem, "Tender," appeared in the Birmingham Arts Journal (Volume 14, Issue 2). My background in English Literature and Psychology informs my writing in poetry as well as in a series of children's books on which I am currently working. My picture book is forthcoming from Mosaica Press and my article on the "K'tonton" books will appear on the *Jewish Action Magazine's* website.

Seth Simons is a writer and entertainment journalist based in the Bay Area. His poems have appeared or are forthcoming in *Rattle, Fugue, Red Wheelbarrow, Breakwater Review, Conduit, Rivet* and the *McNeese Review*. Subscribe to Seth's newsletter (sethsimons.substack.com) and connect with him on Twitter (@sasimons).

Kurt Steinwand These poems are from a chapbook-in-progress titled, Poland, which is an homage to my mother-in-law, who lived her childhood during the Nazi and Russian Occupations of her country. She was reluctant to share any information, so what little she did makes the poems all the more poignant. Thank you for considering these for publication.

Sophia Stid is a poet from California. Currently in the MFA program at Vanderbilt University, she has received fellowships and residencies from the Bucknell Seminar for Younger Poets, Sundress Academy for the Arts, and Signal Fire Arts. She is the winner of the 2017 Francine Ringold Award for New Writers, and was a finalist for the Adrienne Rich Award. Her poems are forthcoming in *Beloit Poetry Journal* and *Nimrod International Journal*.

Allen Sweat is a poet from West Palm Beach, Florida.

Jim Glenn Thatcher is a high school dropout with both a baccalaureate and graduate work in history, and an MFA in creative writing from Vermont College. For most of his boyhood and youth he lived in the only house on a dirt road in the Adirondacks, spending his time in books, the woods, and his imagination —habits that still sustain him. Over the years since then, he has been variously miscast as a soldier, carpenter, steel fabricator, woodworker, pole lineman, laborer, factory worker, and lumberyard hand, among various other livelihoods. Through all of this he has has never lost his deep interest in literature, philosophy, and the idea(s) of history, both natural and human. He has taught at St. Joseph's College, Southern Maine Community College, USM Lewiston-Auburn, and Central Maine Community College, where he was named Poet-in-Residence. His poems have appeared in a number of literary journals and were honored by a 2003 Martin Dibner Fellowship for Maine Writers. He is a former Reviews Editor at *The Cafe Review* and his columns, reviews, profiles and essays have appeared in *Maine In Print*, the *Portland Sunday Telegram, Brunswick Times-Record*, and *Maine Times*, where he was a Contributing Writer. He currently teaches at Andover College.

Barbara Ungar's most recent book, *Immortal Medusa*, was chosen as one of Kirkus Reviews' Best Indie Books of 2015 and won the Adirondack Center for Writing Poetry Award. Prior books include *Charlotte Brontë, You Ruined My Life*, selected by Denise Duhamel for the Word Works' Hilary Tham Collection; *Thrift*; and *The Origin of the Milky Way*, which won the Gival Prize, a Silver IPPY, and a Hoffer award. A single mom and English professor at the College of Saint

Rose in Albany, New York, she has published in the *Southern Indiana Review, Rattle, Salmagundi*, and many others. She has been nominated for the Pushcart Prize five times and was a finalist for Best of the Net.

John Sibley Williams is the editor of two Northwest poetry anthologies and the author of nine collections, including *Disinheritance* and *Controlled Hallucinations*. An eleven-time Pushcart nominee, John is the winner of numerous awards, including the Philip Booth Award, American Literary Review Poetry Contest, Nancy D. Hargrove Editors' Prize, Confrontation Poetry Prize, and Vallum Award for Poetry. He serves as editor of *The Inflectionist Review* and works as a literary agent. Previous publishing credits include: *The Yale Review, Midwest Quarterly, Sycamore Review, Prairie Schooner, The Massachusetts Review, Poet Lore, Saranac Review, Atlanta Review, TriQuarterly, Columbia Poetry Review, Mid-American Review, Poetry Northwest, Third Coast,* and various anthologies. He lives in Portland, Oregon.

Keith Woodruff has a Masters in poetry from Purdue University's creative writing program. He lives in Ohio with his wife Michelle and son Whit, and works from home for a small, virtual marketing company. His work has appeared in *Poetry East, Zone 3, Tar River Poetry, American Literary Review, Quarter After Eight, The Journal, Wigleaf* and is forthcoming in *Juked* and *SunDog Lit*. His prose poem *Summer* appeared in the Best Small Fictions 2017 anthology, and his short short *Elegy* received a 2018 Pushcart Prize.

THE BACK MATTERS

SUBMISSIONS

How to Submit Your Work

From single poems, short stories, and essays to book-length works, novellas, collections, and all experimental spaces in between, NMW + SUNSHOT PRESS + MUSEPAPER is where you want your words to be.

Visit us on the interwebs:

NEWMILLENNIUMWRITINGS.ORG

MUSEPAPER.ORG

SUNSHOTS.ORG

Can't find what you're looking for? Email us:

HELLO@NEWMILLENNIUMWRITINGS.ORG

Colophon Key

1st Place Award Winners 1-139

Title: Azo Sans Uber, Regular, 26 pt | 34 ld
Author: Azo Sans, Bold, 16 pt | 24 ld
Body: Adobe Garamond Pro, Regular, 12 pt | 15 ld

Poetry Suite 139-183

Author: Azo Sans, Regular, 10 pt
Title: Azo Sans Uber, Regular, 16 pt | 19.5 ld
Body: Adobe Garamond Pro, Regular, 10 pt | 13 ld

Sizes are rounded to the nearest .5pt.
Body typefaces usually include multiple fonts (italic, bold, etc.).

INDICTMENT OF TRIDENT

KINGS BAY PLOWSHARES (Plaintiff) vs. UNITED STATES OF AMERICA (Defendant)

INDICTMENT

Today, through our nonviolent action, we, Kings Bay Plowshares—indict the United States government, President Donald Trump, Kings Bay Base Commander Brian Lepine, the nuclear triad, and specifically the Trident nuclear program.

WHEREAS, This program is an ongoing criminal endeavor in violation of international treaty law binding on the United States under the supremacy clause of the U.S. Constitution (Article VI, Section 2):

This Constitution, and the Laws of the United States which shall be made in Pursuance thereof; and all Treaties made, or which shall be made, under the Authority of the United States,

Source: kingsbayplowshares7.org/about/indictment-1/9

shall be the supreme Law of the Land; and the Judges in every State shall be bound thereby, any Thing in the Constitution or Laws of any State to the Contrary notwithstanding.

WHEREAS, The United States is bound by the United Nation's Charter, ratified and signed in 1945. Its preamble affirms that its purpose is to "save future generations from the scourge of war". It directs that "all nations shall refrain from the use of force against another nation". Article II regards the threat to use nuclear weapons as ongoing international criminal activity.

WHEREAS, The Nuremberg Principles, also promulgated in 1945, primarily by the U.S., prohibit crimes against peace, crimes against humanity, war crimes and genocide. They render nuclear weapons systems prohibited, illegal, and criminal under all circumstances and for any reason.

WHEREAS, The U.S. government is obligated as well by the Non-Proliferation Treaty, in force since 1970 that requires the signers to pursue negotiations in good faith and to eliminate nuclear weapons at an early date. The U.S. government is also obligated by the Comprehensive Test Ban Treaty, which prohibits full-scale nuclear explosions.

WHEREAS, the members of the United Nations are currently negotiating a treaty to prohibit nuclear weapons, leading towards their total elimination.

THEREFORE, the work being at done at Kings Bay Naval Submarine Base violates all these agreements and is thus criminal.

Specifically, the Kings Bay Naval Submarine Base refits and maintains submarines, which carry Trident D5 nuclear missiles. The Trident D5 is a submarine-launched ballistic missile (SLBM), built by Lockheed Martin. The Navy currently operates 14 Ohio class submarines. Six have their homeport at Kings Bay. Each submarine carries the capacity to cause devastation equivalent to 600 of the nuclear attacks on Hiroshima, Japan. Thus, the six Tridents maintained at Kings Bay have the capacity to cause the devastation of 3600 Hiroshima-scale attacks.

From the initial mineral mining through testing, storage, and dumping, the production and maintenance of these weapons harms human beings, destroys the environment, and violates international and God's law. Moreover, each day this program steals from all in our nation and world by its theft of much-needed resources. Nor is the Navy or the nation retreating from this violation of international law. The Navy is currently preparing to spend at least $100.2 billion of the public's money on a new class of 12 Trident ballistic missile submarines to replace the current Trident submarines.

Against these continuing violations of treaty law, we assert our right and duty to civil resistance against nuclear weapons. Furthermore, we affirm as crucial the human right to be free from these crimes. The Nuremberg Principles not only prohibit such crimes but oblige those of us aware of the crime to act against it. "Complicity in the commission of a crime against peace, a war crime, or a crime against humanity…is a crime under International Law". The United Nations Charter further reinforced this principle and made it part of the binding international law. Similarly, the Convention on the Prevention and

Punishment of the Crime of Genocide, to which the United States is a signatory, makes it clear that private individuals can be held responsible for acts of genocide.

The ongoing building and maintenance of Trident submarines and ballistic missile systems constitute war crimes that can and should be investigated and prosecuted by judicial authorities at all levels. As citizens, we are required by International Law to denounce and resist known crimes.

For the sake of the whole human family threatened by nuclear weapons, and for the sake of our Planet Earth, which is abused and violated, we indict the Kings Bay Naval Submarine Base and all government officials, agencies, and contractors as responsible for perpetuating these war crimes.

Join distinguished global supporters, including

Noam Chomsky • Medea Benjamin • Michael Moore

Daniel Ellsberg • Rev. Dr. William Barber • Beatrice Fihn

Archbishop Desmond Tutu • other Nobel laureates

and many more

by signing the global petition to dismiss all charges.

Sign the Petition:
http://bit.ly/NMW-KBP7

Donate to the Campagin:
gofundme.com/xaajdf-kings-bay-plowshares-support-fund

I am the great sun,

but you do not see me.

I am your husband,
but you turn away.

I am the captive,
but you do not free me.

I am the captain,
you will not obey.

I am the truth,
but you will not believe me.

I am that city,
where you will not stay.

I am your wife, your child,
but you will leave me.

I am that god,
to whom you will not pray.

I am your counsel,
but you do not hear me.

I am your lover,
but you will betray.

I am your life,
but if you will not name me,

seal up your soul with tears
and never blame me.

—poem found on a 16th Century crucifix

Baba Ram Dass 1931 – 2019
SPIRITUAL TEACHER, PSYCHOLOGIST, AUTHOR
NAMASTE

www.ingramcontent.com/pod-product-compliance
Lightning Source LLC
Chambersburg PA
CBHW030338310726
48979CB00001B/87

9781944977153